D0401064

ATTACK ON PETRA

Attack on
Petra

LEFT BEHIND
>THE KIDS<

Jerry B. Jenkins

Tim LaHaye

WITH CHRIS FABRY

TYNDALE HOUSE PUBLISHERS, INC.
WHEATON, ILLINOIS

Visit Tyndale's exciting Web site at www.tyndale.com

Discover the latest Left Behind news at www.leftbehind.com

Left Behind is a registered trademark of Tyndale House Publishers, Inc.

Published in association with the literary agency of Alive Communications, Inc., 7680 Goddard Street, Suite 200, Colorado Springs, CO 80920.

Edited by Lorie Popp

ISBN 0-8423-5803-X, mass paper

Printed in the United States of America

08 07 06 05 04
8   7   6   5   4   3   2   1

To the Jacobsens:
Jeff, Christian, Joy, Kathryn

And to Ruth Ann, finally home

TABLE OF CONTENTS

THE YOUNG TRIBULATION FORCE

Original members—Vicki Byrne, Judd Thompson, Lionel Washington

Other members—Mark, Conrad, Darrion, Janie, Charlie, Shelly, Melinda

OTHER BELIEVERS

Chang Wong—Chinese teenager working in New Babylon

Westin Jakes—pilot for singer Z-Van

Tsion Ben-Judah—Jewish scholar who writes about prophecy

Colin and Becky Dial—Wisconsin couple with an underground hideout

Sam Goldberg—Jewish teenager, Lionel's good friend

Mr. Mitchell Stein—Jewish friend of the Young Trib Force

Naomi Tiberius—computer whiz living in Petra

Chaim Rosenzweig—famous Israeli scientist

UNBELIEVERS

Nicolae Carpathia—leader of the Global Community

Leon Fortunato—Carpathia's right-hand man

Z-Van—lead singer for the popular group The Four Horsemen

UNDECIDED

Tanya Spivey—daughter of Mountain Militia leader, Cyrus Spivey

What's Gone On Before

JUDD Thompson Jr. and the rest of the Young Tribulation Force are living the adventure of a lifetime. When an attempt to return to the States fails, Judd and Lionel Washington witness an evil musical display in Israel. After Z-Van and The Four Horsemen complete their concert, more people follow Nicolae Carpathia.

Vicki Byrne investigates an intruder outside the Wisconsin hideout and meets Tanya, a teenager in hiding. Vicki tries to persuade the girl about the truth, but she leaves with her brother, Ty.

Sam Goldberg, a young Israeli living in Petra, watches the earth swallow Global Community troops. Later, Sam speaks with Micah, the man who confronted Carpathia in Jerusalem.

Judd and Lionel wait to hear from their pilot friend, Westin Jakes, to see if he will fly them home. A hotel manager announces that anyone not bearing the mark of Carpathia must receive it immediately. As Judd and Lionel pack, they hear a commotion in the hallway. Will they be discovered?

Though Vicki is scolded for venturing outside, she goes out again to leave materials and food for Tanya. Suddenly, a twig cracks nearby. Vicki crouches low and prays.

Sam thrills as Dr. Tsion Ben-Judah speaks to a million people in Petra, but his joy turns to fear as two fighter planes approach the rock-walled city. Have they been wrong about God's protection? Will Nicolae Carpathia annihilate everyone?

Join the scattered Young Tribulation Force as they renew their commitment to following God.

*Rejoice, O heavens! You citizens
of heaven, rejoice! Be glad! But woe
to you people of the world,
for the devil has come down to you
in great anger, knowing that
he has little time.*

Revelation 12:12, *TLB*

ONE

Bombs Away

VICKI shivered—half from a chill, half from fear—and asked God to help her get back to Colin's house. She had hoped to find the cave Tanya had described and place the plastic bag she carried near it. In the darkness, she couldn't locate the cave. The group had obviously hidden the entrance so the Global Community and others wouldn't stumble onto them.

An animal snorted and Vicki nearly screamed. A deer ambled around a tree a few yards away and scanned the area. When Vicki turned on her flashlight, the animal bolted.

She leaned against a tree and put her hands on her knees. Tanya wanted help and Vicki would have gladly given it, but the girl's family was part of some kind of cult. The father's ideas about the Bible seemed weird at best, from what Tanya had said, and Vicki wondered if the girl had thought more about the Bible after their conversation.

Vicki looked at the night sky. The North Star was up there somewhere, but to her it was just twinkling lights. *Judd could find it,* she thought.

Vicki studied the area and chose a path. If she could find something familiar she could work her way back to Colin's house. A few minutes later she turned on her flashlight, expecting to see the gully she had passed earlier. Instead, a series of huge stones blocked her way.

Something rustled to her right, and Vicki scooted closer to the rocks. Another animal? A person?

Vicki gasped as a man holding a gun approached.

Judd Thompson Jr. stood paralyzed in the Jerusalem hotel room. He and Lionel had stayed too long in Israel, and now the Global Community was closing in. Nicolae Carpathia— the ruler the Bible predicted would be the most evil man the world would ever know—was on a rampage against anyone who wouldn't obey him.

A few minutes earlier, a televised message had warned hotel guests that GC personnel would be going room to room to check for anyone without the mark of loyalty.

"What happened to Westin?" Lionel whispered as he packed up the tiny laptop computer.

"He said he was going to inspect the new plane, but maybe he got sidetracked. The GC may have him, or he could be hiding."

Lionel found two baseball caps, and Judd shoved one into his back pocket. If they had to make a run for it, perhaps the caps would hide their foreheads.

The leader of all Carpathia worship, Leon Fortunato, had announced that mark application centers were now open twenty-four hours a day. Anyone without the mark would be forced to take it or face the guillotine. People around the world had lined up early to receive the mark, knowing they wouldn't be allowed to buy or sell anything without it.

Even more bizarre than the mark was Leon's law requiring everyone to worship the image of Carpathia three times a day. Refusing to kneel before a statue meant certain death.

Judd and Lionel had followed Westin Jakes, a fellow believer and pilot for the famous singer Z-Van. Westin had promised to fly them back to the States, but a series of events had prevented the flight. Now, with Westin missing, a sick feeling swept over Judd. Westin was a quick thinker and sharp, but without the mark he was dead.

With their things in two backpacks Westin had provided, Judd and Lionel turned the television off and crept toward the door. They both jumped when an alarm sounded in the hallway, followed by a voice blasting through speakers mounted in the ceiling.

"This is the head of security. We are now making a sweep through the fifth floor in compliance with the Global Community's latest directive. If you do not have the mark of loyalty, you will be escorted to the nearest facility. Please open your doors and move into the hallway."

"What now?" Lionel said.

"Hide."

Sam Goldberg had experienced the highest highs and lowest lows in the past three and a half years. He had lost his mother during the worldwide disappearances. Sam's father had been killed when the horsemen stampeded Jerusalem. And in the temple only a short time ago, Sam had witnessed the murder of his friend Daniel at the hands of Nicolae Carpathia.

But Sam's life had turned around when he believed the message Lionel and Judd had given him. He had peace and a purpose to his life that he had never felt before. His new goal was to convince as many people as possible that God loved them and had sent his only Son to rescue them. Sam had seen miracles on the way to Petra and had heard of many more from people he met there. He had been inches from a chasm that had swallowed a vast army. Then the earth had caved in on itself, as if no tanks or troops had ever been there.

The appearance of an angel was another sign that God was in control and wanted people to rely upon him. God had provided clear, pure water, spouting from rocks around the city, and white wafers on the ground at different times of the day. Quail flew in to provide meat for the people.

God had even supplied those in Petra with computer experts, like Naomi Tiberius, to take over for fallen Trib Force member David Hassid. Everyone grieved David's death, but even with that terrible loss Sam knew e-mails and updates would continue from Petra.

After hearing the booming voice of an angel and seeing the arrival of Tsion Ben-Judah, tears streamed from Sam's eyes. How would he explain these feelings to his friends?

But his elation turned to fear when he heard Nicolae Carpathia was planning to level Petra with bombs. Sam knelt with hundreds of thousands inside Petra as two jets roared in the distance and banked.

Sam knew that if God could open the earth and swallow tanks and troops, he could open the clouds and swallow the jets or cause their instruments to malfunction and send the planes screaming into the ground. But the closer the jets came to Petra, the more Sam feared nothing was going to stop them.

"Please, God, help us!" a woman behind Sam shouted. Her voice echoed off the walls of the ancient city.

A man next to Sam whispered a Psalm. " 'O God, your ways are holy. Is there any god as mighty as you? You are the God of miracles and wonders! You demonstrate your awesome power among the nations. You have redeemed your people by your strength . . .' "

Yes, Sam thought, *you have displayed your power. Will you do it now before it's too late?*

Seventeen-year-old Chang Wong, a member of the Tribulation Force, leaned over his computer and studied the horrifying details. A transmission set up by one of Nicolae Carpathia's top cabinet members allowed the potentate to view every move of the pilots flying over Petra, and Chang tapped into the feed.

Chang had taken over the job left by David Hassid, and as far as Chang knew, he was the only believer in the palace. He had been forced to take the mark of Carpathia but remained a believer, a fact that confused him. Chang hated mirrors and had even tilted his computer screen so he wouldn't see his own reflection.

Working inside the Global Community was a privilege, and Chang knew how important his job was for the success of the Tribulation Force. But part of him wondered how long he could keep up the act. He wished he could go to Chicago and join the safe house in the Strong Building or head to Petra. That was, if Petra survived this attack.

Chang hung his head and breathed a brief prayer. "Father, I believe you are going to save these people from certain death. I don't know how you're going to do it, but I believe in you."

"Praise the name of Carpathia," one of Chang's coworkers said. "May your enemies die!"

"Please gather round," Chang's boss, Aurelio Figueroa, said. He called people to a huge television monitor that showed the same feed Nicolae was seeing. "In just a moment, we will witness the destruction of our enemies."

Vicki stared at the man with the gun and wondered if he had seen her flashlight. He moved behind a rock and Vicki took a breath. A second later an earsplitting blast shook the area.

Before she could cry out, the man ran past her. "Stay here," he said.

He was tall, with a scraggly beard, and reminded Vicki a little of Omer, a friend she had met in Tennessee. He ran into the woods and whistled. Then three young men appeared from behind one of the rocks. Seconds later they dragged a deer's body past her.

"I guess I'd better be going," Vicki said, dusting off the seat of her jeans. "That was a good shot."

"What's in the bag?" the man said.

"Some stuff for a friend of mine. I'll come back another time—"

The man put the gun in front of Vicki, blocking her. "Who's it for?"

Vicki thought about making up an elaborate story, but she decided the truth was best. "Tanya. I met her the other night and thought she could use this. My name's Vicki."

The man didn't offer his name. "I didn't know Tanya had been out again. You'd better come with us."

Though the night was cool, Vicki felt a trickle of sweat down her arms. "I have friends waiting for me. If you'll just tell me which way to the tree line, I'll—"

The man cocked his head. "You came out here to see Tanya, and I'm going to take you to her." He pointed the gun toward the rocks behind her. "Move."

Judd opened Westin's suitcase and threw some clothes around the room. The bed rested on a huge, square platform so they couldn't hide under it. Lionel agreed the closet was a last resort. In the tiny kitchen was an empty space underneath the counter. "Scrunch up in there beside the little refrigerator," Judd said.

Lionel did. Judd walked from the door to the bedroom and noticed Lionel's shoes sticking out.

Footsteps sounded in the hallway.

"Get in," Lionel said. "I have an idea."

Judd knelt and crawled into the space and pulled his feet close to his body. Lionel went to the hall closet, pulled out an ironing board, and set it up in front of them.

"Get one of Westin's shirts," Judd whispered.

"I'm way ahead of you."

Lionel draped the shirt over the board, plugged in the iron, and crawled into the space beside Judd.

A knock sounded at the door. "Mr. Jakes, this is hotel security. Open up, please."

A few seconds later the door clicked and a man walked inside. "Mr. Jakes?"

Judd watched as the shiny, black shoes moved throughout the room. The man went behind the bed, looked onto the balcony, then in the closet.

Another man in a Global Community uniform walked into the kitchen and bumped the ironing board. The man's legs were massive. "Jakes is the one they said doesn't have the mark, right?"

"The filmmaker, Rahlmost, is sure of it," Shiny Shoes said.

"Doesn't look like he's left," Big Legs said. "Still has some ironing to do."

"We can watch the surveillance cameras and catch him coming in," Shiny Shoes said.

"Let's go."

Judd breathed a sigh of relief as the two walked to the front door. Before it closed, the phone rang.

Westin! Judd thought.

Sam couldn't pray anymore, couldn't do anything but watch the huge bombers as they raced toward Petra. People around him whimpered, cried, prayed, and tried to comfort those around them.

"Our God is faithful," Sam finally managed. "We must remember that."

"Amen," someone nearby said.

Sam was about to quote a Scripture he had memorized, but his voice caught as he watched both planes release their bombs at the same time. The deadly payloads looked like they were aimed directly at the center of Petra, at the high place where Tsion Ben-Judah stood.

"Help us," Sam whispered. It was the only prayer he could think of.

TWO

Petra's Fiery Furnace

JUDD prayed for the click of the front door, but the men didn't leave. Instead, they moved back inside and waited. On the fourth ring, the hotel's answering machine picked up. Judd looked at Lionel, wondering what settings were on the phone.

His worst fears were realized when Westin's voice came over the speaker and filled the room. "Judd, Lionel, this is Westin. Pick up if you're there."

Don't say anything about where you are, Judd thought.

"Okay, if you hear this before I reach you, get here fast," Westin said. "The GC are cracking down on people without the mark. There have been some developments with Myron— please, hurry!"

Big Legs moved to the phone and wrote

something on a notepad. "Any idea who Myron is?"

"No, but we might have a bead on the other two, Judd and Lionel," Shiny Shoes said. "We've identified about a dozen people without the mark from surveillance tapes. It could be the young men we spotted—one white, one black."

Big Legs shouted for someone in the hall. "Accompany this gentleman to the security room and take a look at his video archive. We're looking for two younger men—one black, one white—who don't have the mark. Bring me a photo as soon as possible. I'll try to trace this call."

When the door closed, Lionel started to get up, but Judd held up a hand.

They listened to movement in the hall and several people talking. A door slammed, and then the elevator dinged.

Judd nodded and the two emerged from their hiding place. Judd locked the door quietly, then checked the hotel phone and recognized Westin's cell number. Lionel started to pick the phone up, but Judd's cell phone rang. It was Westin.

Judd explained what had just happened. Westin sounded frustrated. "I've got Z-Van on the new plane demanding I fly him and the band to France."

"What for?" Judd said.

"A concert in Paris," Westin said. "The GC is sponsoring a whirlwind world tour."

"Then let the GC fly him," Judd said. "Z-Van will turn you in."

"He could have done that a hundred times by now. Look, I don't want to leave you two hanging—"

"You have to go," Judd said. "Either get out of that plane and run, or fly to Paris and slip away. We'll never make it to the plane before the GC get to you."

"I can try to stall them," Westin said. He explained what the plane looked like and where it was at the airport. "See if you can get here."

Judd hung up and told Lionel what Westin had said.

"You think cabdrivers will care whether we have Carpathia's mark or not?"

"We can't risk it," Judd said. "Wait. Driver. That's it!" He dialed a phone number he had memorized. "You don't know it, but you might have just saved our lives!"

Sam Goldberg watched the bombs hurtling toward Petra and thought about dying. He remembered a quote by some comedian who had said he wasn't afraid of dying—he just didn't want to be there when it happened. Well, Sam was here, and it would be only a few more seconds before the end.

Death meant he would be in the presence of God. After all that had happened during the past few months and years, Sam couldn't wait for that. But he still felt there was more to do, more God wanted him to accomplish.

Sam thought of Judd and Lionel and wondered if they were all right. He recalled friends from his school and neighborhood. The man who owned the pastry shop down the street from their house.

It's funny what you think of when you're about to die, Sam thought.

Sam wouldn't get to meet Chang Wong, Chloe Steele, or any other members of the Tribulation Force. He would never talk personally with Tsion Ben-Judah. At least, not until heaven.

Sam realized he was resigned to his death. He had given up hope that another miracle could save the one million kneeling people in Petra. But if their total destruction was at hand, why had God provided manna and quail to eat and water from a rock? Why had he saved these people from GC attackers? Or sent angels to deliver messages and perform miracles? Why would God go to all that trouble, just to see everyone blown to bits?

Sam relaxed, letting his shoulders droop and tilting his head from side to side. *It will be quick, almost painless*, he thought. An explosion, a flash of fire, and then heaven. Or would there be pain?

Sam's mind flashed to, of all people, Nicolae Carpathia. He and his followers would be joyful that the Israelis and Ben-Judah followers had herded themselves into one area, sitting ducks to Nicolae's war machine.

Sam imagined the news coverage on GCNN the following day. Petra would become a huge plume of smoke and a big hole in the ground. The ancient land of Edom would be the site of the worst one-day holocaust in history, and Nicolae would put on his I-wish-they-would-have-listened-to-me face for the cameras. And he would use this event to convince anyone who hadn't taken the mark to do so.

Sam glanced at Tsion Ben-Judah, who didn't seem concerned. The man watched the descending bombs as if they were a child's kite or two birds flying by. This man had faith, but would that faith be rewarded?

As the warheads neared, parachutes that bore the GC insignia deployed and slowed both bombs. People around Sam whimpered and cried.

Sam noticed black poles attached to the noses of each bomb and asked a man beside him what they were.

The man shuddered. "The GC wants to make sure they do their job. Those sensors will touch the ground and explode the bombs above the surface."

"What does that mean?"

"If the bomb explodes above the earth, it is more effective."

"You mean it will kill more of us?"

"Yes. We are doomed."

The bearded man led Vicki between two rocks and pointed to a small opening hidden by some bushes. Vicki squeezed through the darkened area, put out her hands to steady herself, and touched both sides of the cave. She recognized the smell of damp earth, the same smell as on Tanya's clothes.

After inching a few feet farther, she neared an area lit by a small lantern. The narrow passage widened into a larger room. Empty crates and cartons were stacked along the wall, and a series of tunnels led away from the room.

Tanya stepped out of one of the tunnels and gasped. "Vicki! What are you—?"

Vicki held out the plastic bag. "I brought you some things. I felt guilty we weren't able to talk more."

Tanya looked at the bearded man and approached Vicki. "We're both in a lot of trouble."

Mark rubbed his eyes and walked into the computer room. Vicki was nowhere in sight, and he guessed she had gone to the bathroom. He turned the volume up on the television to hear a GCNN special report.

The news anchor stared into the camera with a grim face. ". . . and sources tell us that an aerial attack is now under way that is meant to deal with several million armed enemies of the Global Community. They are hiding in a mountainous region discovered by ground forces in the Negev Desert."

"Petra," Mark whispered. He called for Vicki, but there was no answer.

"The rebels have reportedly murdered countless GC troops and have taken over tanks and armored carriers. In an effort to root out this threat, Global Community Security and Intelligence Director Suhail Akbar has announced that two warheads are being dropped as I speak, and another missile is on its way to—" The man put a hand to his ear and nodded. "We're getting a report of a live feed from one of the planes. . . ."

A picture of the underside of a plane flashed on the screen. Below, the unmistakable city of Petra gleamed in the sun. Two specks were visible in the center of the picture.

Mark held his breath as the screen flashed white, and then a red-and-black cloud of billowing smoke rose from the floor of the desert. God had not spared Petra like the Tribulation Force had believed, and Mark couldn't imagine the horror on the ground.

"What you're seeing now," the news anchor droned, "is the death of what one Global Community official estimates at 90 percent of the rebels, including their leader, Tsion Ben-Judah."

Chang Wong stood with his coworkers before a television monitor and watched the live feed as the fighter-bomber circled above Petra. The pilot reported that his mission had been accomplished and suggested the missile launch was unnecessary.

Chang's boss, Aurelio Figueroa, chuckled.

"The rebels aren't rebels anymore. Look at that. The pilot has to fly even higher to stay away from the smoke."

The launch sequence started for the missile and Chang wondered why. No one could have survived the first blasts. He went through the mental checklist of Tribulation Force members in Petra. Rayford Steele, Tsion Ben-Judah, Chaim Rosenzweig—or Micah as he was now known, and others were there along with a million followers.

Chang wanted to race to his room and contact the Trib Force in Chicago, talk with Judd or anyone else who would listen. Would the Young Trib Force be the ones to rally believers and reach out to people with the message of God's love?

As people around him made jokes about the "crispy rebels" and the "mostly nuclear" weather forecast for Petra, Chang clenched his teeth. He had long thought about where he would go if he escaped New Babylon. Now, Petra wasn't an option.

Sam saw a white flash and covered his head, expecting the force of the blast to throw him into the air before his body disintegrated. He rolled into a ball on the ground and screamed as the explosion boomed through the red rock city.

Thousands screamed with Sam, wailing and shrieking at their hopelessness in the face of such terror. He expected rock formations to crash down or the heat of the explosion to vaporize his skin, but the shock wave didn't knock him down and the heat didn't burn.

It took a few seconds, but Sam finally opened his eyes and saw the most horrific sight of his life. His body was on fire! He guessed that his nerve endings had been burnt, but when he pinched himself, he felt it. His sense of smell hadn't left him either. The stench of the fire filled his nostrils and made him gag, but the hair on the back of his arm was still there. He felt his head and found hair there as well.

Flames were so thick that he could see only a few feet around him. Everyone was on fire. Was he in the middle of a horrible dream, a pre-death vision of some sort, or was it really happening?

Was he in hell?

Flames shot high above him. This was a lake of fire the likes of which the world had never seen.

Suddenly, a few yards ahead, Sam saw a robed man stepping over burning bodies.

White, yellow, red, and orange flames burst from his beard, his hair, and his robe. The man's face was on fire, but instead of his skin melting and being consumed, he kept walking, as if he were walking underwater wearing weighted boots.

Mr. Stein! Sam thought. *Maybe this is what we must go through just before we reach heaven!*

But it was not heaven. They were still in Petra.

"Samuel!" Mr. Stein called, using Sam's full name. As he came closer, the man smiled.

"What happened?" Sam yelled over the noise of the deadly blaze.

"Deliverance," Mr. Stein shouted. "The Lord has seen fit to deliver us, not by stopping the flames, but by walking through them with us!"

THREE

Tsion Speaks

ALL AROUND Sam, people stood, staggering under the unreal sight. Everything was on fire. People. Their clothes. Rocks. Bushes. Even the air burned. It was like living inside a furnace.

And yet, they were *living!*

The surging flames blotted out the sun. Some people raised hands to the heavens. Others embraced. Instead of crying, wailing, and pleading with God for safety, Sam heard laughter.

Mr. Stein reached Sam and held out a hand. Fire danced from the ends of his fingers. Sam did the same, mirroring Mr. Stein's movements. He held a hand close to his face and tried to blow out the fire, like candles on a birthday cake, but still the flame sizzled on his skin.

Mr. Stein hugged Sam. "I knew God would provide."

"How can we hear each other?" Sam said over the inferno.

"If God can save us from this blaze, he can certainly let us hear each other!"

A man bumped into Sam and laughed, his beard billowing fire. "Sorry about that, son!"

"It's okay," Sam said. Then he laughed. How silly for a man who had just been bombed to apologize for bumping into someone!

Mr. Stein grabbed Sam's hands and danced in a circle. "You remember the story of the children of Israel in the fiery furnace?"

"Shadrach, Meshach, and Abednego," Sam said.

"Yes. When the king looked into the fire, he saw four men instead of those three. The Lord was walking with them, giving them victory and safety."

"I wonder what the king of the earth can see when he looks into this furnace," Sam said.

And they continued to dance.

Mark glanced at the clock as he gathered the others in the main room. It was just after four in the morning. Shelly looked for Vicki as the others watched live coverage of the Petra bombing.

"I can't imagine what those people went through," Becky Dial said.

"We can take comfort in the fact that it was quick," her husband, Colin, said. "No one could have survived it."

GCNN showed live video of the scene. A huge mushroom cloud lifted, and white-hot flames shot a thousand feet in the air.

"We understand that the Global Community has confirmed their launch of a missile from Amman, Jordan," the anchor said. "It should be arriving at this site momentarily. Let's give you some background now on this group that was targeted today. . . ."

As the anchor showed video footage of Tsion Ben-Judah, Conrad shook his head. "I can't believe they're sending a missile after blowing Petra to smithereens."

Mark felt a lump in his throat. Dr. Ben-Judah's messages had been part of his daily routine for such a long time. Now there would be no encouraging words from this man of God.

"I don't get it," Becky said. "If God didn't protect all those people . . ."

"Go ahead," Colin said, "finish your thought."

"Well, how can we trust him to keep his

other promises? Was the Tribulation Force misreading the Bible?"

Colin put his arm around his wife and hugged her. "There has to be some explanation, but for the life of me, I can't figure it out."

Sam giggled and snorted in the midst of hundreds of thousands who danced, sang, and screamed praises to God. People formed circles, linking arms, dancing, and hopping wildly. Old men, young men, frail women—everyone celebrated another deliverance by God.

"Praise the God of Shadrach, Meshach, and Abednego!" someone shouted.

Sam had heard of fire raining from heaven, but this seemed to bubble up, engulfing everyone in and out of Petra.

Sam was torn away from Mr. Stein by a group of young people who skipped into the flames. They gathered others as their line lengthened, snaking through the crowd. When they reached a plateau, Sam recognized Naomi, the computer whiz, and broke free.

"Isn't this something?" Naomi yelled over the celebration.

"It's wonderful!" Sam said.

"I'm just worried about the computer

equipment," Naomi said. "A blast like that had to affect it."

"We can get new equipment if we have to," Sam said, grabbing her hands. "Let's celebrate!"

Naomi laughed as Sam swung her in a circle. Sam liked the way Naomi smiled. He flung his head back and looked at the sky, but he couldn't see past the flames surrounding them. The marks on the believers' foreheads near Sam seemed to glisten in the glow of the surging fire.

"It feels too good to be true," Naomi said. "I want to tell Chang about this."

Naomi rushed into the crowd to find her father, and Sam noticed a teenager curled up on a fiery rock, his knees pulled to his chest. The boy held a hand close to his face, studying the yellow flames licking his fingertips. Sam drew closer and saw the boy had no mark on his forehead.

"You're safe," Sam said softly.

The boy looked up, eyes wild like an animal's. "I don't understand. How can we be burning and still be alive?"

"It is the work of almighty God," Sam said. "He has protected us."

The boy stared. "Then why didn't he protect my little brother and sister during the disappearances? Why didn't he save my mother from the earthquake? Or my father from the poison gas?"

Sam tried to comfort him, but the boy stood. "I don't want anything to do with a God like that," he said angrily.

"Then why did you come here?" Sam said.

"Because I heard there might be answers. I listened to Micah in Masada, but he never talked about this!"

The boy wandered into the flames. Others without the mark cowered and wailed. Even with so much evidence of God's power, some would simply not believe.

A voice called out above the noise. "People! People! People!" It was Tsion Ben-Judah. "There will be time to rejoice and to celebrate and to praise and thank the God of Israel! For now, listen to me!"

Even Tsion's voice could not totally quiet the crowd. People stopped dancing and singing, but many still hugged each other and laughed.

"I do not know," Dr. Ben-Judah began, "when God will lift the curtain of fire and we will be able to see the clear sky again. I do not know when or if the world will know that we have been protected. For now it is enough that we know!"

People cheered and clapped. It sounded like Tsion was close, but Sam couldn't see him.

"When the evil one and his counselors gather," Tsion continued, "they will see us on whose bodies the fire had no power; the hair of our heads was not singed, nor were our garments affected, and the smell of fire was not on us. They will interpret this in their own way, my brothers and sisters. Perchance they will not allow the rest of the world to even know it. But God will reveal himself in his own way and in his own time, as he always does.

"And he has a word for you today, friends. He says, 'Behold, I have refined you, but not as silver; I have tested you in the furnace of affliction. For my own sake, for my own sake, I will do it, for how should my name be profaned? I will not give my glory to another.

" 'Listen to me, O Israel,' says the Lord God of hosts, 'you are my called ones, you are my beloved, you I have chosen. I am he, I am the First, I am also the Last. Indeed, my hand has laid the foundation of the earth, and my right hand has stretched out the heavens. When I call to them, they stand up together.

" 'Assemble yourselves, and hear! Who among them has declared these things? The

Lord loves him; he shall do his pleasure on Babylon. I, even I, have spoken.'

"Thus says the Lord, your Redeemer, the Holy One of Israel: I am the Lord your God, who leads you by the way you should go. Oh, that you had heeded my commandments! Then your peace would have been like a river, and your righteousness like the waves of the sea. Declare, proclaim this, utter to the end of the earth that the Lord has redeemed his servants and they did not thirst when he led them through the deserts. He caused the waters to flow from the rock for them; he also split the rock, and the waters gushed out."

Sam thrilled at Tsion's voice. As the fire raged, he wondered if anyone else knew what was happening in Petra.

Vicki leaned against a cave wall as several members of the group came to meet her. They stared without speaking, then scowled at Tanya as if she were a criminal.

"What trouble are we in?" Vicki said when the others moved away.

"I convinced Ty not to tell anyone I went to your place."

"I couldn't leave you out here alone," Vicki

said, handing her the bag with food and materials. "I'll leave this and go."

"You don't understand. You can't leave. My father made the rule. Anyone who comes in must stay until Armageddon."

Vicki gasped. "That's more than three years away. He can't keep me here."

A hush fell over the room as a man walked through one of the larger tunnels with a huge torch.

Tanya trembled. "It's my father."

Chang Wong tried to keep his cool, tried not to show emotion as GC workers cheered the news from Petra. The techies quieted as the pilot flying over Petra reported that he could see the missile headed for the red rock city.

One of Chang's coworkers, Rasha, pointed to the right of the screen. "There it is!" A trail of white smoke followed the rocket across the screen, headed straight toward the inferno.

Chang's boss clasped his hands. "This is the end of our troubles with those pesky Judah-ites."

The missile entered the black cloud. Chang had hoped there might be some survivors on the outskirts of the city, but if the missile was as big as Chang had heard, no one within miles of Petra would survive.

The explosion sent a shock wave so strong that the plane's camera reacted seconds later. The fire expanded, swallowing more land. Chang could hardly watch, while the others seemed glued to the monitor.

"Wait, what's that?" Rasha said.

The pilot's voice cut through the static. "I'm seeing—I don't know what I'm seeing. Water. Yes, water. Spraying. It's, uh, it's having some effect on the fire and smoke. Now clearing, the water still rising and drenching the area."

"Well, that will make it easier for the GC forces to go in there," Mr. Figueroa said, but the pilot continued his transmission.

"It's as if the missile struck some spring that, uh—this is crazy, Command. I see—I can see . . . the flames dying now, smoke clearing. There are people *alive* down th—"

The feed quickly cut out, and Chang's coworkers groaned.

"That can't be!"

"No one could survive that kind of—"

"Two bombs and a missile? No!"

Others cursed and leaned against desks, clearly upset at the possibility that God had come through again.

Chang stifled a smile. He couldn't wait to

get back to his computer to hear the conversation between the pilot and the officials in New Babylon.

"Yes!" Mark screamed, raising a fist in the air. "Yes, yes, yes!!!"

"They're alive!" Colin yelled as he hugged his wife. Everyone wept at the news that people were alive in Petra. GCNN broke into the coverage and said they were having technical difficulties.

Conrad gave Mark a high five. "I'd give a boatload of money to hear what Nicolae Carpathia is saying right now."

Shelly came back downstairs, and Mark told her the good news. She smiled but seemed distracted.

"What's wrong?" Mark said.

"It's Vicki. I can't find her anywhere."

Sam heard something whistling overhead, and the ground shook with a huge explosion. Fire whooshed by him, like a giant had blown out a burning match. Another sound followed, like the rushing of a thousand horses, but as the fire and smoke left, he saw water gushing from a massive hole in the earth. Sam looked at his watch and counted a full minute before the water cascaded back to the ground.

The fire and billowing smoke disappeared and instead of flames licking at Sam's fingers, cool, fresh water fell over him like a spring rain. People reached toward heaven, their palms raised and their faces turned to the sky. God had used the missile to turn on a fountain that spread refreshing water to everyone.

Sam spotted Tsion Ben-Judah and Chaim Rosenzweig standing next to the geyser and ran toward them. He wondered why some people were still weeping while others danced, hugged each other, and shouted praises to God.

As he ran, Sam laughed.

FOUR

Tanya's Father

VICKI had wondered what Tanya's father looked like. She pictured the man as tall with a commanding personality, someone others would follow into a hole in the ground and stay for three years. But this man wasn't anything like that. He was short and round, with a squarish face and long sideburns. He wore a one-piece outfit that zipped up the front. Vicki gripped his pudgy fingers as he greeted her.

"Welcome to the Mountain Militia," he said. "I'm Cyrus Spivey. I hear you already know my daughter."

Vicki nodded. "I brought her some food and a few things to read."

Cyrus smiled and introduced the others in the cave.

"If it's okay, I'd like to go back to my

friends now," Vicki said. "They'll be worried about me."

Cyrus's belly jiggled as he laughed. He put an arm around Vicki and guided her to the larger entrance. "Your friends will be all right. Come on, I want to show you the place."

Mark ran a hand through his hair. The elation of discovering people alive at Petra was crushed by the news that Vicki was gone.

"She promised she wouldn't go out again," Colin said.

"Maybe someone took her," Shelly said.

Mark slammed a fist on the computer table. "That's it. She may have a good reason, and she might have thought we'd never find out, but if she's not going to live by the rules, she'll have to leave."

"Mark!" Shelly said. "Vicki's one of the reasons the Young Trib Force exists. You can't just shove her out."

"If she's a danger to the group we can, and we should."

Colin stood and rubbed his chin. "We'll decide if we need to do anything after we find her. Let's search the house again and make sure she's not here."

Mark looked over his shoulder at the television as he climbed the stairs. The GCNN was in chaos trying to cope with the possibility that people had survived the explosions in Petra.

Sam ran close to the enormous waterspout. Instead of destroying Petra, the missile had caused water to burst from the ground and douse the fire.

Sam glanced at Tsion and Chaim. It looked like the two were trying to get people's attention, but it was useless. People pranced about in the rain, shouting, singing, and rejoicing.

"Praise be to the God who sees us through the fire!" one man yelled.

"Thank you, God, for sending the water to quench Nicolae's flames!" another shouted.

Hundreds of thousands raised their hands toward heaven, welcoming the water that cascaded onto them. But Sam couldn't figure out why some wept. Were these unbelievers like the young man he had met earlier? Why had God protected them? Did he know they would eventually turn to him?

A few minutes later, the people calmed and turned their attention to Dr. Ben-Judah. The water's roar was deafening, like standing at the edge of a waterfall, and Sam wondered if he would be able to hear Tsion. When the man spoke, it was as if Tsion were standing right beside him.

"I have agreed to stay at least a few days," Tsion said. "To worship with you. To thank God together. To teach. To preach. Ah, look as the water subsides."

As if someone had flipped a switch, the surging water slowed and Sam saw the top of the gusher. It shrank slowly to earth until it gurgled and bubbled into a small lake. Sam turned his gaze toward Dr. Ben-Judah.

"Some of you weep and are ashamed," Tsion said. "And rightly so. Over the next few days I will minister to you as well. For while you have not taken the mark of the evil one, neither have you taken your stand with the one true God. He has foreseen in his mercy to protect you, to give you yet one more chance to choose him.

"Many of you will do that, even this day, even before I begin my teaching on the unsearchable riches of Messiah and his love and forgiveness. Yet many of you will remain in your sin, risking the hardening of your heart so that you may never change your mind. But you will never be able to forget this day, this hour, this miracle, this unmis-takable and irrefutable evidence that the God of Abraham, Isaac, and Jacob remains in control. You may choose your own way, but you will never be able to disagree that faith is the victory that overcomes the world."

Sam glanced at those still weeping. He wondered if the young man he had spoken to earlier would accept the truth about God or reject him.

Judd and Lionel pulled their baseball caps down and stood by the front door of the hotel room. Judd had called Sabir, the former terrorist turned believer who had recently driven them from Tel Aviv to Jerusalem. Sabir said his wife had gone to Petra, but he had stayed in Jerusalem.

While they were speaking, news came of the bombing of Petra. Judd prayed with Sabir, then rejoiced as the pilot reported there were actually people alive on the ground.

"Why didn't you go with your wife?" Judd asked.

"I sensed I should stay. Perhaps someone is in trouble, I thought. Perhaps there will be people who will need to hear the message of forgiveness one more time."

Judd explained what had happened and

that they desperately needed to get out of the hotel.

"I'll come immediately," Sabir said. "I'll call when I'm close."

Judd nervously checked his phone every few seconds to make sure he didn't miss Sabir's call. The hallway remained quiet with no GC Peacekeepers or Morale Monitors passing. Lionel turned on the news, but GCNN only showed replays of the first explosions in Petra.

Lionel switched to the hotel's channel, which repeated the announcement that everyone needed to take Carpathia's mark. Judd's phone rang and he answered quickly. It was Chang Wong. Judd put the call on speakerphone so Lionel could hear.

"Get your people to pray," Chang said. "It looks like the Petra operation was a flop for Carpathia."

"We saw the coverage," Judd said.

"I haven't listened to the recording inside Nicolae's office yet, but I wouldn't be surprised if he tries something else. Plus, have your people pray for a rescue operation in Greece."

Lionel opened the laptop and typed a message as Chang and Judd talked. Judd explained their situation and Chang seemed concerned. "There are no believers working

inside the GC in your area that I can find.
You should either hide with your friend in
Jerusalem or try to get out. Things will be
very bad for believers in the coming days."

Judd's phone blipped, and Chang said he
would pray for them.

Judd punched in the call and heard Sabir's
voice. "I am at the front of the hotel. There
are people lined up along the street to take
the mark of Carpathia."

"It would be suicide to come out the
front," Judd said. "There have to be side exits
in a building this big."

"There are Peacekeepers and Morale Monitors at each exit."

"Fire escape?" Judd said.

"Also guarded."

Judd looked at Lionel. "We're trapped. If
we go out any exit, they'll stop us."

"Then we must pray," Sabir said.

Vicki stooped as she walked through the
entrance into the main meeting area of the
Mountain Militia. Every few feet the group
had placed posts to support the roof. Though
there was very little light, Vicki adjusted to
the dark and found the area musty but warm.

Through another crevice was the supply

room, where a dwindling number of canned goods was stored. Vicki learned that each family had a sleeping area and its own supply of food and water.

Cyrus put his torch in a crude holder carved out of the rock. "We've had to ration lately, but that should end soon."

Two young men with bloody hands brought in pieces of deer meat and passed through the room.

"I suppose we'll have a feast for dinner tonight, Mr. Spivey," a boy said.

Cyrus smiled. "We eat dinner when most people are eating breakfast. We have to limit our movement during the daylight hours." He held out a hand. "Please, sit."

Vicki sat on a wooden crate of tomato soup. "Won't cooking that meat create a lot of smoke?"

"Good question. There's a kitchen in the back. Once a day we cook things on an open pit with ventilation in the ceiling. The smoke rises in a clump of evergreens above us."

"You guys have thought of everything."

Cyrus scratched his chin. "Including what to do in case anybody ever stumbles onto this place." He looked at Tanya. "Or if one of us disobeys."

"I'm sorry, Dad," Tanya said.

"Did Ty know about this?"

"I made him promise not to tell you."

"My own kids. I never thought it would happen that way." He put his hands on his knees and rubbed back and forth. "Okay, here's the situation. I've been listening to the radio, about the attack on Petra—"

"Petra's been attacked?" Vicki said.

"It's been wiped out along with everyone in it. The timetable is coming true. Armageddon can't be more than a week or two away. A month tops."

"But Dr. Ben-Judah said Petra was the place of refuge. Are you sure?"

Cyrus nodded. "God's going to set up his kingdom with the faithful, and we're going to be part of the 144,000. You'll stay here until that comes true. If you want to become one of us, that's fine. It's your choice."

Vicki's mind reeled. If Petra had been bombed and the Jews and Judah-ites killed, Tsion was wrong.

"Tanya, show Vicki where she'll sleep after dinner," Cyrus said.

Vicki stood, but instead of following Tanya, she turned to the group's leader. "I came here to help your daughter with food for her body as well as her soul. I believe you're wrong about God and the timing of everything. In fact, I know you are. I'd like to tell you about him, and I'd like to see you get supplies. We're not even close to Armageddon. It's more than three years away. And I promise you, whether you believe what I'm going to tell you or not, I won't tell the GC about this place. But you can't keep me here. I have to get back to my friends and the others who are depending on me."

Cyrus's face flushed. "Are you finished?"

Vicki nodded and he motioned at Tanya to take Vicki away. "In the Old Testament they stoned children for talking back to their parents. You're not our child, but you're under our roof now. We'll decide what's to be done."

Judd held the phone at his side and took a breath. Sabir had just asked God to help them make it to the airport before Westin left, but Judd figured Z-Van and his plane were long gone.

Lionel had come up with the plan, including cuing Sabir to the exit they would take out of the building. Judd wished he could send Vicki a final message before they set the plan in motion, but there wasn't time.

Judd had felt God's protection the past three and a half years. He had survived

everything from the wrath of the Lamb earthquake to fiery hail and more. Would this be
how his life would end, caught in a hotel in
Jerusalem without the mark of Carpathia? He
was prepared to give his life if he were
caught.

Lionel lit a match to a newspaper and held
it above his head. The flames and smoke rose
toward the ceiling. An alarm screamed in the
room and hallway. Then the sprinkler system
went on, dousing the flames and everything
in the room. Lionel threw the scorched paper
in the nearest sink and ran for the door.

Judd held the phone under his jacket,
watching through the peephole. Several
people ran toward the elevators, then turned
for the stairs.

"Number two," Judd shouted in the
phone. "Exit number two!"

Judd opened the door and pushed Lionel
into the hallway, pulling his cap low on his
forehead and praying their plan would work.

FIVE

Escape

LIONEL tensed as they moved into the stairwell. Several people rushed ahead of him. He
and Judd hoped to blend in with the rest of
the crowd as they pushed out of the hotel,
but there was no telling how the GC would
react.

As the fire alarm buzzed, more people
jammed into the stairwell. A mother holding
a screaming baby squeezed between Judd
and Lionel. When they reached the first floor,
Lionel found himself in a mass of people
struggling to get out.

"Slow down!" a Peacekeeper up ahead
said. "Don't panic!"

The Peacekeeper and two Morale Monitors
studied the crowd as people hurried through
the door. Lionel sidestepped and let the
woman with the baby pass. He tried not to

make eye contact with anyone as he approached the door.

"We think it's just an alarm, not a real fire," one of the Morale Monitors said.

How do they know that? Lionel thought.

"If you were staying on the fifth floor, please move to the side," the Peacekeeper said. Someone from behind pushed Lionel to the middle of the pack. He was about ten feet from the door when the Peacekeeper said, "Okay, stop right here."

People behind Lionel grumbled. One man coming down the stairs yelled, "What's the holdup?"

"Just checking for the mark of loyalty," the Peacekeeper said. "Have you out of here in a minute."

Judd moved next to Lionel and started coughing. Lionel picked up the cue and both coughed. Finally, Judd said in a hoarse voice, "I smell smoke. . . ."

The baby wailed as the woman pushed ahead. "I need out!"

People panicked. A Morale Monitor blew a whistle, but the crowd surged, pushing the officers back. Lionel was carried through the doors and onto the sidewalk. He saw Sabir's car and ran to it.

Sabir waved wildly as Lionel jumped in the

back. He expected Judd to join him but he
didn't.

"Back there," Sabir said, pointing toward
the hotel.

Judd lay at the bottom of a pile of people
on the ground. GC workers tried to help as
people pushed and struggled.

"We have to do something," Lionel said.

Going out the door, a man beside Judd had
tripped and fallen. As Judd tried to help him
up, someone bowled them over and a chain
reaction started as frantic people scrambled
out of the building.

The Peacekeeper moved toward the door
while the two Morale Monitors tried to untan-
gle the pile. In the scuffle, Judd's hat flew off
and one of the Morale Monitors grabbed
Judd's hair and pulled his head back.

"You have no mark!" the Morale Monitor
said.

As the young man pulled a whistle from
his pocket, Judd rolled out of the pile and
pushed him. The Morale Monitor, stunned,
lost his balance and fell, the back of his head
striking a decorative stone by the sidewalk.

"What did you say, Roy?" the other Morale
Monitor said, coming around the pile.

"He's hurt," a woman said. "That guy pushed him."

Judd retrieved his hat and jammed it down hard. "It was an accident."

The other Morale Monitor rushed to his injured friend. A horn honked and Judd saw Lionel and Sabir. Everything seemed in slow motion as Judd walked away.

"You there, stop!" the Peacekeeper yelled over the crowd.

In a daze, Judd kept going. Sabir pulled up and Lionel swung the back door open. As they pulled away, the Morale Monitor was still motionless on the ground.

Mark and the others at Colin Dial's house searched for Vicki and found nothing but some missing food. Mark opened the last print job from the computer and found pages from the kids' Web site on how to become a believer. He pulled up the video recording from the cameras and spotted Vicki walking into the woods.

Colin called everyone together. "If she doesn't come back by daylight, we need to go after her. She could be lost."

Mark crossed his arms. "I think we need to figure out what to do when we find her."

"We don't know why she left," Shelly said. "Let's just find her and go from there."

The computer beeped, alerting them to a new message. Colin opened it and found a note from Darrion Stahley.

I was up late watching the Petra coverage and thought you guys could use some information for the Web site, Darrion wrote. Attached was a document detailing what had happened in Petra and a transcript of what the pilot had said.

Mark was impressed. He wrote a few more notes for the file and placed the document on the Web site along with links on how to become a true believer. When he had finished, he thanked Darrion and asked her to pray for Vicki.

Vicki sat on the dirt floor of a room Tanya and her family had blocked off from the others. Tattered covers hung on a clothesline separating their section of the cave from the rest of the group. Wooden crates blocked another section. When Vicki asked what it was, Tanya told her it was the spot where the earthquake had covered an entire family.

Tanya sat beside Vicki. "You shouldn't have crossed my dad like that."

"I wanted to be straight with him. I came here to help you, and I need to leave after you've heard me out."

"Look, it's all going to be over soon and we can get out of here. Why do you want to cause trouble?"

Vicki scooted closer and lowered her voice. "It's not going to be over soon. Like I told your dad, we have more than three years left before Armageddon."

"But he said they were bombing that place—"

"Petra, I know. But if I'm right, those bombs will miss their mark or somehow the people will survive."

"How do you know?"

Vicki pulled a Bible and some notes from the plastic bag. "I'm not going to push this on you if you don't want to hear it."

"Go ahead."

Judd stared out the window as Sabir drove through alleys and backstreets. They didn't think the Peacekeeper was close enough to read the license plate on Sabir's car, but they couldn't be sure. Sirens sounded a few streets away, but they didn't see any GC patrol cars until they reached the main road to the airport.

"Why are you taking us there?" Judd said.

"Lionel said this was your way out of the country," Sabir said.

"But Z-Van's plane has to be gone by now."

"Sabir's been praying," Lionel said. "We should too."

Judd glanced at Lionel. "We should pray for that Morale Monitor at the hotel. I might have killed him."

"I saw what happened," Lionel said. "You didn't mean to hurt him."

"Yeah. So why doesn't that make me feel any better?"

Sabir began praying aloud, asking God to protect Judd and Lionel and get them safely back to the States. When he finished, Judd asked if they could stay with him if the plane ride didn't work out.

"I will help in any way I can," Sabir said.

Judd phoned Westin as they came in sight of the airport. Voices blared as Westin picked up.

"Wes, it's Judd. Are you in the air?"

"Negative. We've had a little delay here. Where are you?"

Judd told him.

"You won't believe this," Westin said. "We were just about to take off when the plane malfunctioned. Everybody had to get off so the mechanics could do their job."

"What's the problem?" Judd said.

Westin lowered his voice. "There's a switch in the cockpit that disables the generator to the engines. Took the mechanic a while to find out that I had *accidentally* hit both switches. They're almost finished fixing the pin and Z-Van wants back on."

"I can see the airport now," Judd said. "You have room for two more?"

Vicki began with the basics about how to have a relationship with God.

Tanya frowned. "I don't understand. My dad says God's really ticked off at the world for being so bad. That's why he's killing everybody during Armageddon."

"God is angry at the evil in the world," Vicki said, "but his judgments are to wake us up to the truth. He wants people to give their lives to him and accept his forgiveness. That's why he sent his Son."

"Jesus?"

"Right."

"My dad says Jesus was a great prophet. He was going to set up his kingdom on earth, but when people killed him, God left that job up to us."

Vicki scratched her head. "Does your dad believe Jesus came back from the dead?"

Tanya shrugged. "I guess so. He says we all come back in some form or another. If we've done more bad stuff than good, we come back as an animal or some kind of plant. If we've done more good than bad, God lets us into heaven or we become angels."

Vicki couldn't believe the strange things Tanya's father believed. Whatever they were, they weren't from the Bible.

"That's why Dad is so mad about me going to your place," Tanya continued. "He doesn't want me messing up my chance to see Mom again."

"What happened to your mother?"

Tanya grabbed a handful of dirt from the floor and sifted it through her fingers. "She and my dad got into some big fights just before it happened. She'd been listening to some radio station, and they'd sent her some stuff to read."

"Stuff about God?"

"I guess so. Dad's never talked about it, only to say that there wasn't a better woman in the world and he's sure she made it to heaven. It's up to us to do enough good stuff so we can all be together."

"What happened to her?"

Tanya looked at her blackened fingernails. Smoke from the burning meat a few rooms away wafted into the area. "Dad woke up that morning and she was gone. Her nightgown and wedding ring were beside him." A tear streaked down Tanya's cheek. "I try really hard to be good, but I'm scared I'm gonna come back as a goat or a lilac or something."

Vicki put a hand on her shoulder. "You don't have to be scared. I can tell you right now you won't come back as any of those things. In Hebrews it says that a person dies only once and after that comes the judgment."

"That's not what Dad says. Show me."

Vicki opened the Bible and turned to Hebrews, chapter 9 and read the verses aloud. " 'And just as it is destined that each person dies only once and after that comes judgment, so also Christ died only once as a sacrifice to take away the sins of many people. He will come again but not to deal with our sins again. This time he will bring salvation to all those who are eagerly waiting for him.' "

"So we only die once?" Tanya said.

"Right. Then God judges you."

"And if our good outweighs our bad . . ."

Vicki shook her head. "God can only live with something pure. If we have any sin at all, we can't get to heaven."

Tanya rolled her eyes. "I guess that leaves me out."

"Me too. And everybody else. We've all sinned and deserve to be separated from God forever. The good news is that God made a way for us to be perfect."

"That doesn't seem possible."

"Jesus was the only person who ever lived a sinless life. He was more than just a prophet. He was God's Son. And like it says in that verse, he died as a sacrifice to save people. If you ask him to forgive you, he will. Then God doesn't look at your sin—he sees the perfection of Jesus."

"This is what Mom believed, isn't it?" Tanya said.

"I think so."

"Then why didn't she tell me?"

"Maybe she didn't have the chance."

Tanya stood as her brother walked in. "You two are supposed to come to dinner."

Tanya reached out a hand and helped Vicki up. "You have to talk to my dad. I'm not sure he'll listen but try."

"What about you?" Vicki said, but Tanya had already turned and was leading her through one of the darkened tunnels.

SIX

Vicki's Message

VICKI took her seat on a packing crate at a small table. Others crowded around or sat against the wall balancing plates on their knees.

The deer meat was brought on a wooden slab with a huge hunting knife sticking out of it. As a woman placed it before Tanya's father, several people clapped. Vicki had told her friends back home that she would never eat "Bambi," but she had to admit a gnawing hunger.

Cyrus folded his hands and closed his eyes. "We thank you, God, for providing, and we ask you to bless the new challenge we have with your wisdom. Amen."

Cyrus cut the meat into large chunks and handed it out. Vicki's portion was about half the size of her hand. She tore off a small piece, trying hard not to think of the deer. The meat tasted a little salty but was tender.

"Tanya says you have something to tell us," Cyrus said, turning his attention to Vicki.

Vicki wiped her mouth and began. "I'm sorry I offended you by talking so strongly. I'm a little scared. My friends didn't want me to go out again, but I had to talk with Tanya one more time."

"So there are two daughters of sin in the room?"

Others laughed and Vicki smiled. "I guess you could say that. I've been interested in what Tanya says you teach about the Bible."

"Mmm. You're open to truth, then? Good." Cyrus pointed toward a crude black-board at the front of the room. "Every morning—which is actually evening to you—we meet in here at breakfast and go over something of God's plan."

"Prophet Cy's a great teacher," a man said. "You can learn a lot from him."

"What did you talk about today?" Vicki said.

"The final battle. Once it's over and the kingdom is set up, we'll be going outside to the new heaven and new earth. This is what we've prepared for. Since we're part of the righteous who survived, we'll take our part in

building that kingdom. Today we went over
some of the duties the righteous will have."

"Vicki has a different idea," Tanya said.

Vicki gave Tanya a look, breathed a quick
prayer, and put her fork down. She began
with her story, how her parents had become
"religious" just before the disappearances.
When she found her family gone, she and
some others discovered the truth. Jesus
Christ had come back for his followers and
had left everyone else behind.

"I saw a video of a pastor talking about
what he believed was going to happen," Vicki
said. "I was scared because everything he said
had come true."

"What did he say?" Tanya said.

Vicki noticed people had stopped eating
and leaned closer to hear. "It's been a while
since I've seen it, but I remember how he
started. He said something like, 'I can imagine what kind of fear and despair you're
going through as you watch this tape.' He
had recorded it especially for those left
behind."

Vicki closed her eyes and saw the face of
the senior pastor of New Hope Village
Church, Vernon Billings. She remembered he
sat on the edge of the desk as he spoke.

"The pastor said that anyone who had

placed their faith in Christ alone for salvation had been taken to heaven," Vicki continued. "Then he showed us how he knew what was about to happen." She looked at Cyrus. "Do you have a Bible?"

Cyrus handed her one but instead she asked him to read some verses from 1 Corinthians. He had trouble finding the passage, but when he did, his voice was strong and clear as he read the words that had changed the course of Vicki's life.

" 'But let me tell you a wonderful secret God has revealed to us,' " Cyrus read. " 'Not all of us will die, but we will all be transformed. It will happen in a moment, in the blinking of an eye, when the last trumpet is blown. For when the trumpet sounds, the Christians who have died will be raised with transformed bodies. And then we who are living will be transformed so that we will never die. For our perishable earthly bodies must be transformed into heavenly bodies that will never die.'

" 'When this happens—when our perishable earthly bodies have been transformed into heavenly bodies that will never die— then at last the Scriptures will come true:'

" ' "Death is swallowed up in victory.
O death, where is your victory?
O death, where is your sting?" ' "

" 'For sin is the sting that results in death, and the law gives sin its power. How we thank God, who gives us victory over sin and death through Jesus Christ our Lord!' "

Silence followed. Finally, Tanya said, "I don't get it. What does that mean?"

"The pastor explained it like this," Vicki said. "When Jesus came back for his true followers, those people were given new bodies, and they were reunited with him. That's what happened during the disappearances. The pastor also said that children would be taken, even the unborn from their mothers' wombs."

A woman in the back gasped, then ran out of the room.

After a pause, Vicki continued. "The pastor also predicted that people would have heart attacks because of the shock of losing family members so quickly. He said others would commit suicide. And he was clear to say that the disappearances weren't the judgment of God. He said this time period is God's final effort to reach out to those who have rejected his way. He's calling every person alive into a relationship with himself.

"The pastor went on to predict that a ruler would rise who promised peace. This man would gain a great following, and many would believe he was a miracle worker."

"Carpathia," Cyrus whispered.

"Yes. He will be a great deceiver, won't keep his promises, and will speak out against God. The pastor on the tape predicted a war that would kill millions and a great earthquake."

The room was quiet. People hung on every word. Vicki knew the next section of the video asked people to respond.

Here goes, Vicki thought.

Judd handed the phone to Sabir, and Westin directed him to the correct airport entrance. "Your friend is radioing a guard to let us through," Sabir said.

Once inside the gate, Sabir maneuvered close to the hangar, where mechanics hurried around Z-Van's new plane.

Judd and Lionel thanked Sabir again for his help. "I feel bad leaving you," Judd said.

Sabir shook Judd's hand a final time. "Stay strong in the Lord. If you ever need me, please call."

Judd and Lionel slipped inside the plane without being seen by anyone in the terminal, and Westin quickly showed them his quarters. "I'd give you the grand tour, but Z-Van is hot to make it to Paris for tonight's concert."

The cabin was toward the front of the plane and had a fold-out bed, a closet, and a desk area completely outfitted with the latest technology. Pullout drawers were big enough for Westin's clothes, and the room even had a small bathroom and shower.

"I'm going to lock the door from the outside," Westin said. "Nobody will be able to get in, but you won't be able to get out."

"We'll stay quiet," Lionel said.

"Oh, and one more thing," Westin said. "There's a little present on the computer you might have fun with."

Westin left and locked the door. Judd sat at the computer and noticed a camera icon in the corner. He brought up the picture and saw each room of the plane. Judd looked around the cabin, making sure there was no camera looking in on them. Seeing everything going on in Z-Van's plane would make the flight even more interesting.

Vicki took a drink of lukewarm water and sat back. The people were clearly interested in what she was saying, but Tanya's father looked more and more uncomfortable. He ate the venison and kept a wary eye on the rest of the group.

"What did the video say then?" a woman asked.

"Keep in mind, this was before Nicolae Carpathia even came to power," Vicki said. "Everything the pastor said was right on target. God's Word, the Bible, doesn't lie. He said that government and religion will change, war and death and destruction will come, and believers in God will be killed because of their faith."

"Did he say why we were left behind?" a man said.

"He said the main point is that those left behind missed the truth. But the good news is, God's giving us a second chance."

Cyrus put his fork down and looked at the others. "You all know that Beelzebub is at work in the world, and he has his disciples spreading doctrine of demons. I've taught you from the beginning that God punishes the wicked. Our job is to do the right thing. And I think the right thing is to keep this little Jezebel locked up where she can't hurt anyone else."

Vicki knew the man had lots of power over these people. But instead of feeling scared, she was more confident.

"You can read this for yourself," Vicki said. "The pastor on the tape quoted Ezekiel 33:11, where God says, 'I take no pleasure in the death of wicked people. I only want them to turn from their wicked ways so they can live.' "

"The God we pray to is a jealous God. He's angry at people for their sin."

"But don't you see," Vicki pleaded. "God hates sin, but he loves people enough to die for them. Remember the parable Jesus told about the son who went away and wasted all his father's money?"

"The Prodigal Son," someone behind her said.

"Yes, that's it. But one of the main points of the story Jesus told was the love of the father for his rebellious son. He waited and waited, and when the boy finally came home, he didn't punish him. He prepared a great feast and welcomed him. That's the kind of love God has for every one of us if we'll accept it."

Some in the group grumbled, siding with Tanya's father. Others seemed interested in Vicki's message.

"If what you're saying is true," Tanya said, "our hiding in here has been senseless. We should be out there with you telling as many people as we can."

"Enough," Cyrus said. He motioned to an older man. "Take these two to the room. I'll deal with them later."

Vicki and Tanya walked behind the kitchen to the only place in the underground labyrinth with a door. The man handed Tanya a lit candle and locked them inside.

"This is where they put us if we've done something against the group," Tanya said.

"No wonder everybody obeys," Vicki said, glancing around. "I don't want to be locked up here either."

Tanya sat on an empty crate, and Vicki found a place close to her.

"I think I understand what you're saying," Tanya said. "I've always thought of God as upset with me. You know, looking down from heaven, shaking his finger."

"Like your father," Vicki said.

Tanya nodded. "But the way you talk about him makes me think God really cares."

"Your mother understood that," Vicki said softly. "I know she wanted to tell you."

"Is it too late for me?"

Vicki smiled. The face of the pastor on the tape flashed in her mind. He had looked both concerned and compassionate, knowing the people seeing the tape would be scared and upset. "I'll tell you the prayer the pastor on that tape prayed, as well as I can remember. It's simple. You can pray it with me if you mean it."

Tanya knelt on the dirt floor and closed her eyes. "I'm ready."

As Vicki prayed, Tanya repeated her words. "Dear God, I admit that I'm a sinner. I am sorry for my sins. Please forgive me and save me. I ask this in the name of Jesus, who died for me. I trust in him right now. I believe his blood paid the price for my salvation. Thank you for hearing me and receiving me. Thank you for saving my soul."

Vicki helped Tanya to her feet when she was finished. "The Bible says that if you confess with your mouth that Jesus is Lord and believe in your heart that God raised him from the dead, you will be saved."

Vicki held the candle close to her own face.

Tanya gasped. "What's that?"

"The mark of the true believer. God places this on everyone who calls on him during this time."

"That's how you knew I wasn't genuine," Tanya said.

"Right."

Tanya sat down hard on the crate. "Now I have to convince my father and the others, but I don't think it's going to be easy."

71

Vicki put a hand on the girl's shoulder. "No matter what happens with them, I promise you this. You'll see your mom again."

SEVEN

Flight to Paris

JUDD and Lionel kept quiet as Z-Van and his followers filed onto the plane. Z-Van yelled and cursed at Westin for taking so much time, then started toward the back. "Oh," the singer said, "you'll be taking the mark when we get to Paris. Wouldn't want you out of GC code."

Westin glanced at the hidden camera and winked.

When a woman Judd didn't recognize climbed aboard, Z-Van got everyone's attention. "I want you to meet Gabrielle. She'll be our backup pilot for Westin, should anything happen to him." He smiled and Judd felt a chill. Was Z-Van planning something in Paris?

"Strange," Lionel said. "Z-Van hasn't needed a backup pilot before."

As the plane took off, Judd quickly wrote

Chang Wong in New Babylon and explained how he and Lionel had escaped the GC. He told him where they were going and asked for the latest on the Tribulation Force.

A few minutes later Chang wrote back and told Judd he had checked the hotel's database. *They have a picture of you and Lionel headed out of your room, but your hats block your faces. Good job. They also tried to follow the car, but no one got a clear look at the license.*

There is some confusion about what happened outside the building, Chang continued. *A Morale Monitor is in critical condition at an area hospital. What happened?*

Chang revealed that in addition to helping the Tribulation Force with their rescue assignment in Greece, he was also trying to locate his sister, who was on her way to China. *I think she's trying to find my parents to make sure they are all right. Pray for her.*

Chang finished his break and walked back to his desk. Coworkers with grave faces went about their jobs. Chang had kept his distance with the others. It was difficult enough pretending to be loyal to Carpathia to his boss let alone those he sat near each day.

The person at the next desk, Rasha,

scooted her chair near Chang and spoke softly. "What do you think of Petra?"

"What do you mean?"

"Those bombs hit the target. The missile too. So why did we cut the transmission when the pilot thought he saw people moving?"

"Could have been animals or something."

Rasha frowned and pulled Chang toward her computer screen. "I have a satellite image up of the area."

"Do you have clearance for that?"

Rasha gave him a look. "What are you going to do, rat on me? Look at those dots. Something's moving down there." She scrunched her face, and the wrinkles in her forehead made Nicolae's mark bunch into a weird shape. "This is creepy. First we lose contact with all those military people. Who knows where they went. Today we drop precision bombs that should have turned Petra into a dust bowl, but I can still see the rock formations."

Chang had listened to conversations at the watercooler and around the office and wondered if any of his coworkers had ever considered God. Now, with the mark of Carpathia on every forehead, he grieved for them. He wasn't any different than any of these people, except that God had broken through and convinced him of the truth.

"I'll be glad when this day is over," Rasha said.

Chang nodded and returned to his desk. Unlike the others, he had been thrilled to hear there were people alive on the ground. He shuffled papers on his desk, pretending to work, then picked up the silver Nic sitting atop his computer screen, a replica of Carpathia encased in a plastic cube. His boss had presented it to him to recognize Chang's work with the convoys of equipment, supplies, and food from Global Community sources. What the GC didn't know was that Chang had designed his system to cause delays and even send some food and supplies to the Tribulation Force Co-op.

Chang typed some gibberish to make it look like he was busy as several high-ranking GC officers walked by his desk.

One spoke into a cell phone. "Tell him the second pilot is on his way. We'll have him in his office as soon as possible."

Chang activated the bug in the office of Suhail Akbar, chief of Security and Intelligence. He would have to wait until later to hear what Akbar said to the men.

It had been four hours since Mark first awakened to find Vicki gone from the Wisconsin hideout. Shelly had kept constant watch on the video screens, hoping Vicki would return. Conrad had e-mailed several key people in the kids' database and asked them to pray. Colin and Becky brought some fruit and cereal for breakfast, and Mark told them they hadn't heard anything from Vicki.

"I know we're all upset," Becky said, "but Vicki wouldn't endanger us. She has a good heart."

Mark shook his head. "She's always stressed that we're a team. What does it do to the team if people go off by themselves?"

Conrad turned from the screen. "We have more than a hundred people praying for her."

Colin and the others knelt and asked God to lead Vicki back to the house or help them find her. "We don't want to take unnecessary risks, but we need your help," he prayed.

Mark felt so angry he couldn't pray. When they finished, Colin asked Mark and Conrad to get their things and follow him upstairs. Becky and Shelly would monitor the cameras and communicate by radio if they saw movement.

Conrad stopped Mark as they reached the outside door. "Maybe it's not my place to say anything—"

"Just say it."

"I heard you set off on your own a while ago."

Mark looked at the floor. "I was stupid. I got involved in the militia that thought it could stand up to GC forces. Almost got myself killed."

Conrad nodded. "Did the group welcome you back?"

"Judd and Vicki were upset, but they knew how bad I felt."

"We all make mistakes. I guess I'm asking that when we find Vicki you'll try to treat her like she treated you."

Mark pursed his lips. "I'll think about it."

Sam felt giddy all day, singing along with the thousands who celebrated God's deliverance. People danced around the pool of water, some slipping in to get their feet wet and splashing around. Others jumped in, drank freely, and swam. Many who did not have the mark of God sat, too stunned to speak.

The pool of water in the middle of the desert was another sign of God's goodness.

How could anyone not believe? How could anyone live through the consuming fire they had seen that morning and still have doubts about God?

Sam found Naomi at the busy computer center. "The electromagnetic pulse from just one of those bombs should have fried every hard drive in this building," Naomi said. She pointed toward the flickering screens around the room. "As you can see, not one of them was taken out."

"Incredible!"

"I'm beginning to train people to staff this place," Naomi continued. "Some will do simple data entry, others will forward messages already created, and some will answer questions about the Bible, theology, or practical matters. Will you help me find candidates?"

Sam smiled. "If you'll let me sit in on your training, it'll be my pleasure."

Vicki looked at her watch and realized it was after eight in the morning. Being inside the cave had already affected her. The ground was cold and the air musty, but her time with Tanya had been good, talking about what the Bible said was in store for each believer.

Tanya was thrilled about the Glorious Appearing of Jesus Christ, but she was saddened by the death and suffering that would occur before that event.

As fatigue set in, Vicki closed her eyes and put her head against the cool cave wall. Sleeping during the daytime wouldn't be that difficult, since there was no daylight, but Vicki wondered how the group had gotten used to the closed-in feeling.

"I think I've decided something," Tanya said as Vicki was nodding off. "I think I should help you get out of here."

"What about you?" Vicki said. "You should come with me."

"I don't think so. At least not yet. I need to let my dad and the others see the difference in my life. They can't see my mark, but they should be able to see a change in me."

Vicki laughed quietly. "God's light in a dark place. Perfect."

"What's the best way to reach out to my dad?"

Vicki shook her head. "Your dad's beliefs are a strange mixture of all kinds of things—the Bible, reincarnation, and stuff I've never heard of. The Bible says the truth will set you free. It did for you and your mom. We just have to pray that he and the others will see the truth before it's too late."

Tanya nodded. "Okay. Get some rest. I'll come up with a plan."

Judd settled in on the flight to Paris, opening a window on the computer screen to monitor Z-Van and his gang, then writing the kids in Wisconsin about their plans. Lionel folded the bed out quietly and fell asleep.

When Judd tried phoning Westin to talk about his fears concerning Z-Van, he couldn't connect. He tried to get an update on Petra, but the Global Community News Network avoided the topic.

Judd checked Tsion Ben-Judah's Web site, but there was nothing new. Judd would have to simply believe Tsion and the others in Petra were all right and wait to hear his message.

Something on the screen caught Judd's eye, and he clicked the video feed. Z-Van's musicians sat at the back of the plane, their backs to the camera. A video played on a huge monitor that stretched nearly the width of the entire plane. Judd zoomed in on the picture, plugged headphones into the monitor, and turned up the volume.

Leon Fortunato stood before Z-Van, his hands outstretched. Judd had seen this look on Fortunato's face twice before. The first had been at the funeral for Nicolae when Leon had called down fire from heaven. The second was in Jerusalem when the evil man had killed Hattie Durham, a member of the Tribulation Force.

Leon's eyes flashed and his face contorted with a sick, twisted smile. "As the father has given to me, so I now give to you. The harvest is abundant, but the workers are few. On behalf of our lord and god, I send you as a worker in the fields. Go and reap followers—make disciples of Lord Carpathia in every nation. Use your music, your talents, your showmanship to draw all people unto him, so that he will be lifted high."

Z-Van trembled as Leon put his hands on the singer's head. "All authority has been given to me," Leon said, "and I now pass that authority onto you to do great and marvelous things the world has yet to see."

Judd thought about Tsion's teaching that Satan was the great imitator. He wanted so much to be God that he would counterfeit the Lord's work.

Z-Van scanned the faces of his musicians. Judd switched views and noticed each person stared directly ahead, no blinking.

When the video ended, Z-Van stepped in front of the monitor. "You have seen what the Most High Reverend Father of Carpathianism has given me. You saw a little of my power onstage in Jerusalem. Tonight, you will see even greater things. Tonight, in front of hundreds of thousands, we will win the hearts of many, turn them to the true lord, and make a sacrifice to our king."

Z-Van put out his hands and those seated went rigid. He whispered something, then opened his eyes, red as flame, and let loose an evil laugh.

EIGHT

Search for Vicki

MARK and the others wore clothes that blended into the Wisconsin countryside. They followed Vicki's footprints into the woods but lost the trail a few yards in. They spread out and headed north.

"Sure wish we had Phoenix," Conrad said into his radio. "He'd find her."

"Keep quiet," Colin said.

Colin had shown them a series of hand signals they could use to communicate. Mark walked as quietly as he could, checking for any sign of a cave or underground dwelling.

When they came to a ravine, Mark signaled the others. "Let's check down there and make sure she didn't fall. She could have slipped over the edge in the dark."

The three worked their way to the bottom where a small stream ran through jagged rocks. Mark sighed with relief when they found nothing, and Colin led them back up the hill.

Conrad looked at his compass and the three set off again.

Judd put his head in his hands. He hated watching Z-Van onstage and hearing his songs that glorified Nicolae Carpathia. But something Z-Van had just said repulsed Judd even more. What was the man going to do? Did it involve Westin? Judd wished he could go to the cockpit, but he couldn't get out of the room and didn't dare try.

Judd quickly wrote an e-mail to Chang Wong detailing what he had seen. He sent the message and checked the rest of the kids' Web site. There were new messages coming in, many asking for an explanation about Petra.

I thought Tsion Ben-Judah said Petra would be safe, one person wrote. *What does this mean for believers throughout the world?*

Judd fired off a quick response. *Don't be so sure about Petra. Before the pilots were cut off, they saw something on the ground.*

Judd checked the GCNN site and found nothing about survivors. He sat back and thought about the Morale Monitor he had hurt at the hotel. Judd couldn't get the young man's face out of his mind. Should Judd pray for him? Just because he had the mark of Carpathia didn't mean he wasn't a human being.

Is this what it will be like the rest of the Tribulation? Meeting people with the mark of Carpathia and knowing they'll never accept the message of Christ?

"God, I admit I don't know what to pray about that guy," Judd prayed honestly. "I didn't mean to hurt him. You know who he is and I know that you're kind and merciful. Please reach one of his family members or someone near him through the pain of this injury. Amen."

Vicki couldn't tell what time it was when she awoke, but she tasted grit in her mouth. She had been in Tanya's world less than twenty-four hours and didn't think she could stand much more.

These people are pretty committed to what they believe if they've stayed here all this time, Vicki thought.

The candle wasn't lit and Vicki strained to find Tanya in the inky blackness. A thin strip of light shone under the door, and Vicki was surprised to find it unlocked. The light outside bathed the room. Tanya wasn't inside.

She crept through the kitchen into the tunnel that led to the eating room. Voices came from somewhere ahead.

"Get your guns," Cyrus said. "This is a red alert."

Vicki rushed through the tunnel and found the frantic group. The men had assembled at the front, light showing through the tunnel entrance.

"Vicki!" Tanya called from behind her.

"Quiet," Cyrus said. He looked at his son, Ty. "Get her back to the room."

"What's going on?" Vicki said.

"Keep your voice down. There are people outside. Might be GC. We're not taking any chances."

"It could be my friends!"

Tanya's father clamped a hand over Vicki's mouth and shoved her toward Ty.

Mark spotted the rocks first but didn't think much about them until he saw a path worn into the wooded area. He knelt to inspect it and signaled to Colin and Conrad.

"No footprints," Mark whispered. "What's making this?"

"Maybe animals," Colin said. "There's a water source nearby, but the path leads up to the rocks."

"Guys, over here," Conrad whispered. He pointed to dark brown spots in the dirt. "Is that blood?"

Colin knelt and touched the spots. "Looks like it."

"You think they've hurt her?" Mark said.

"Maybe she was attacked by an animal," Conrad said.

The three followed the blood trail up the path, nearing several huge rocks.

Vicki struggled against Ty as he led her to the back room. Finally she broke free and turned. "I'm not going to scream."

"How can I trust you after what you told my sister?"

"She talked to you about what she believes?"

"She wouldn't stop. You told her she would see Mom again."

"That's what the Bible teaches."

Ty shook his head. "I don't know what to think. A lot of people have followed Dad. You know what it means if he's wrong?"

"It means you have a chance to believe what's right," Vicki said. "You're all really committed, but you have to be committed to the truth."

Ty leaned against the side of the cave and sighed.

"Is there another way out of here?" Vicki whispered.

"I can't tell you that. There could be GC out there right now. They'd catch you."

As she talked, Vicki moved behind Ty and inched closer to the tunnel. "Where's Tanya?"

Ty turned and Vicki bolted toward the entrance, now surrounded by Mountain Militia. A gun clicked as she hurried through the narrow passage.

"Did you hear that?" Mark whispered. The three had walked around a weird-shaped rock. "Sounded like a voice."

They stopped and listened. "I didn't hear anything," Colin said.

They walked around the edge of the rock and into a gully on the back side. "Should we climb it?" Conrad said. "Maybe there's some kind of opening on top."

Colin shook his head. "People couldn't come and go that way. Let's check the blood trail one more time."

Vicki pleaded with the men to put their guns
away. Ty arrived and Cyrus smirked. "You let
a girl get away from you?"

"My friends are out there, not the GC!"
Vicki said.

The man with the long beard returned.
"There's three of them. Civilian clothes. No guns."

"You'd better hope for their sakes they
don't find you," Cyrus said.

"Let me go. I promise we won't—"

The bearded man clamped a hand over
Vicki's mouth and took her to the back of the
cave. She was crying when he placed duct
tape across her mouth and around her wrists
and ankles. Tears streamed down Vicki's face
as the man laid her on her side and locked
the door.

Mark searched for the blood trail but
couldn't find it. "I swear it was right here."

Colin raised his voice. "There's nothing
here, guys. Let's head back to the house."

"But—"

"Come on," Colin said firmly.

Mark trudged through the woods, stopping
when he thought he heard a muffled scream,

then hurried to catch up with Colin and
Conrad.

Judd woke Lionel as a new report came over
GCNN.

The news anchor spoke over video of Petra
burning. "We have a report just in from
Global Community headquarters in New Babylon. The two planes that dropped their
payloads over Petra earlier today have reportedly been shot down by rebel forces on the
ground. The bodies of the pilots were discovered in the Negev this afternoon. Due to pilot
error, their payloads missed the target by more
than a mile, and the insurgents fired missiles
that destroyed both planes. The Global
Community expresses its sympathy to the
families of these heroes and martyrs to the
cause of world peace."

As they watched more coverage, Judd told
Lionel what Z-Van had done in the back of
the plane. Lionel shook his head.

A quick check of the Web site yielded
another message from Chang.

> *I'd get away from Z-Van. I just heard a
> conversation between Carpathia and
> Fortunato that made the hair stand up on
> the back of my neck.*

*First, news about Petra. Tell everyone
there is life in the city! The head security
and intelligence guy here, Suhail Akbar,
actually had the two pilots who dropped the
bombs in his office. They're dead, but the
news won't say that Akbar had them killed
to cover up the truth.*

*I've been tracking my sister and helping
with the rescue in Greece, but what I heard
from Carpathia stopped me. The Global
Community will reward anyone who kills a
Jewish person anywhere in the world.
Carpathia wants Jewish people tortured and
imprisoned as well.*

Judd gasped as he read. If Carpathia
wanted to do that to Jews, what would he do
to followers of Christ?

*Let me give you the transcript of what
Nicolae told Leon Fortunato. I think this
will explain Z-Van's actions.*

Pasted onto the document in a different
font was the back-and-forth conversation
between Nicolae and the leader of his religion, Leon Fortunato.

Carpathia: Stand up, Leon, and
hear me. My enemies mock me. They
perform miracles. They poison my

people, call sores down on them from
heaven, turn the seas into blood. And
now! And now they survive bombs
and fire! But I too have power. You
know this. It is available to you,
Leon. I have seen you use it. I have
seen you call down lightning that
slays those who would oppose me.
Leon, I want to fight fire with fire. I
want Jesuses. Do you hear me?

Leon: Sir?

Carpathia: I want messiahs.

Leon: Messiahs?

Carpathia: I want saviors in my
name.

Leon: Tell me more, Excellency.

Carpathia: Find them—thousands
of them. Train them, raise them up,
imbue them with the power with
which I have blessed you. I want
them healing the sick, turning water
to blood and blood to water. I want
them performing miracles in my
name, drawing the undecided, yea,
even the enemy away from his god
and to me.

Leon: I will do it, Excellency.

Carpathia: Will you?

Leon: I will if you will empower
me.

Carpathia: Kneel before me again, Leon.

Leon: Lay your hands on me, risen one.

Carpathia: I confer upon you all the power vested in me from above and below the earth! I give you power to do great and mighty and wonderful and terrifying things, acts so splendiferous and phantasmagorical that no man can see them and not be persuaded that I am his god.

Leon: Thank you, lord. Thank you, Excellency.

Carpathia: Go, Leon. Go quickly and do it now.

If I'm right, Leon gave some kind of power to Z-Van before his concert in Jerusalem. But these messiahs Nicolae speaks of are going to be very different. More powerful and even more dangerous.

NINE

Z-Van's Tricks

JUDD monitored Z-Van as the singer huddled with the others and went over the order of the show. One band member asked about instruments, and Z-Van assured her they would have the normal setup.

As the plane neared the airport, Judd glanced out the window. Many of the familiar sites on the Paris skyline had been destroyed during World War III. The Eiffel Tower, probably the most famous spot for foreign visitors, had been leveled. But as soon as Nicolae Carpathia was fully in power, he had most of the bombed buildings and landmarks rebuilt. Of course these new points of interest had the unique signature of the Global Community.

As darkness fell, they flew close enough to see the Arc de Triomphe, another stunning

site. Leon Fortunato had recently ordered
that Nicolae's statue be displayed at the top
of this monument so people could fulfill
their daily worship.

Thousands lined the sidewalks in front of
the statue. Judd couldn't believe after all the
miracles and signs from God that people
were still willing to follow Carpathia. God
had given so many chances to believe the
truth, but people chose against him.

A steady stream of people headed toward
bright lights. In the distance were thousands
jumping and rolling in a human sea before a
stage. At other concerts there would be a
warm-up band, but Z-Van allowed no one
onstage before him.

Lionel called Judd to the computer as
Westin perfectly touched down on the
runway.

Z-Van had just gotten off the phone with
someone at the stage. "We're all set," he said.
"Three limos are waiting. It should take
fifteen minutes to get there." He looked at
his watch. "They have our clothes backstage
so we're on in less than half an hour."

"When will the . . . you know . . . when
will that happen?" the drummer said.

Z-Van curled his lips and hissed, "It
happens when it happens. The timing will be
perfect." He beckoned the others to stand,

and they joined hands. Z-Van lifted his face toward the ceiling. "Lord Carpathia, we know your spirit is with us, and we ask you to empower us to bring more people to you tonight. We know there will be others coming after us who will do mighty things in your name, and we thank you that we can play a small part in helping your cause."

The others in the circle grunted their approval. Judd glanced at Lionel, who looked shocked and disgusted.

"Lead others in the path of power that you have shown us," Z-Van continued. "And may those who do not serve you turn today or reap their reward. May they feel the blade upon their neck this very night."

"Yes!" others said. "The blade."

Something banged and Judd switched camera shots. Westin had opened the outer door.

Z-Van finished the prayer, nodded to the others, and the group moved forward. Band members exited without a word or glance at Westin. A group of fans waited outside, chanting and screaming.

Z-Van was the last in line and paused at the door. "Come with us tonight."

"I'll head over after I finish with the log and get the place cleaned up," Westin said.

The singer snapped his fingers, and the backup pilot reentered the cabin. "Let Gabrielle take care of the details. You come with us."

Judd turned to Lionel. "They're trying to trick Westin."

"Yeah, but what are they planning?"

Z-Van put an arm around Westin. "We want to dedicate tonight's show to you."

"Don't do it," Judd whispered through clenched teeth.

Westin pulled away. "I'll be there. Just let me finish here and—"

"I simply won't take no for an answer," Z-Van said. He gestured to someone outside the door.

"What are you doing?" Westin said.

"I told you, you're coming with us."

Two burly men grabbed Westin and hustled him out the door.

"Why?" Westin yelled. "I've done nothing but good to you."

Z-Van smirked. "And I'm finally going to do something good for you. I know why you have refused to take the mark, Judah-ite."

Judd felt trapped. He wanted to help Westin, but they were behind a locked door.

"Tonight you'll have the chance of a lifetime," Z-Van said, "to take the mark in front of thousands of adoring fans."

"I'll never do it!"

"Sad. Then it will be your last chance to see us in concert. And tonight you will be the main attraction."

The two men pushed and pulled Westin down the ramp.

Z-Van turned to Gabrielle. "I'm sorry you had to see that, my dear. Don't worry about filling out any useless logs. Familiarize yourself with the plane, take it for a spin if you'd like, and be ready to take us to Madrid when we return."

"Will Westin be with you?"

Z-Van ran his tongue over his lower lip. "Unless something extraordinary happens, you won't be seeing him again, except on GCNN."

With a laugh, Z-Van swept out of the plane to the screams of fans.

Mark couldn't believe Colin was giving up the search. Several times Mark tried to talk with him, but each time Colin held up a hand and continued walking.

When they reached Colin's house, Mark followed him downstairs and grabbed his arm. "You've been good to us, but what was that about? I think Vicki's back there!"

"Calm down," Colin said. "I think she's there too, but that was not the time to rescue her."

"You think she's near the rocks?" Conrad said.

"I'm sure of it. The stuff Tanya told us—the animal blood and the fact that they're running out of food. It all fits."

"You found blood?" Becky said. "How do you know it's not Vicki's?"

"I think they're holding her," Colin said. "I heard a gun click. If we'd have snooped around more, they might have shot at us."

"Who are these people?" Shelly said.

"Probably just as mixed up as we were before we heard the truth," Colin said. "I have a plan, but we have to wait for nightfall."

Mark looked at his watch. He wondered if Vicki could hold out that long.

Vicki lay in the dark with her hands taped behind her back. She strained to hear voices, but the door was shut. She was sure Mark and the others had been outside. She was glad she hadn't heard gunfire, but she wasn't sure she could hear it from the locked room.

Vicki felt something brush against her face and immediately struggled to sit up. She shook her head and sat for a moment. She felt the movement again and thought it might be a spider. Then she realized it was her hair moving against her skin. A draft came from somewhere. Under the door?

Vicki worked the tape back and forth, but it was wrapped around her wrists several times. She sat back and closed her eyes. If these people had gone underground, were there others in hiding who weren't Carpathia followers? If so, could the Young Trib Force reach them?

Vicki rested her head against the dirt floor and tried to sleep.

Judd watched the limos pull through the gate by the tarmac. Lionel knelt by the bed, his face in his hands. Judd joined him, and the two prayed for Westin and for guidance about what to do.

When they finished, Judd stood. "We have to help him."

"I'm good to go," Lionel said, stuffing things into their backpacks. "But how do we get out of this room?"

Judd tried to pull the door open quietly, but it was solid. There were two screws in the back of the lock. "If we had a screwdriver we might be in business."

Lionel pulled out a small pocketknife. "Will this work?"

Judd opened the blade and fitted it into one of the screws. The blade was too small. Lionel rummaged through the drawers and found a pair of tweezers. Judd bent them until one blade tore free. He stuck the other in the hole and it fit perfectly, but the screw was too tight to turn. He tried the other screw and managed to get it started.

Footsteps passed through the hallway so Judd stopped. The handle jiggled. He heard keys and held his breath. Lionel clicked the camera icon on the computer and saw Gabrielle standing by their door. When she had tried every key, she gave up and moved to the back of the plane.

Lionel brought Westin's razor from the shower stall. By wedging it into the device he managed to get enough leverage to turn the screw. A few minutes later Judd gently pulled the door handle toward him. Half the mechanism fell into his hand.

The door flung open. Gabrielle held the other end of the door handle. "What are you doing here?" She was dark haired and slim, with the mark of Carpathia on her forehead. On her lapel was a clip-on pass identifying her with The Four Horsemen.

Judd peeked around her and noticed the plane's door was still open.

"Who locked you in there?" she said. "Was it Westin?"

Judd and Lionel looked at each other, not saying anything. The woman tried French, but they kept quiet.

"Wait here," she said, turning to the cockpit.

Judd and Lionel took the opportunity and raced past her. When she turned, Judd snatched the pass on her vest and bolted down the stairs.

Judd and Lionel ran forward. Fans remained by the gate, and their screams drowned out the yells from Gabrielle. Security officers stepped from their small building.

"We missed the limos!" Judd yelled, waving the pass over his head. "Open the gate."

A security officer glanced at the plane, pointing at Gabrielle who had fallen on the stairs and waved from the ground.

"She's telling you to open up," Judd said. "Z-Van will be ticked if we don't get to the concert quick!"

The man shrugged and opened the gate. About a hundred fans mobbed Judd and Lionel, thinking they were with Z-Van. They ran away from the gate with the crowd. Lionel asked if anyone had a car nearby, and two ladies screamed and grabbed his jacket. Judd followed and they squeezed into a tiny car.

"Are you really with The Four Horsemen?" a woman said with a heavy accent.

"We flew with them from Jerusalem," Judd said. "Can you get us to the concert?"

The driver smiled and jammed her foot to the floor. "Right to the door."

Judd and Lionel kept quiet, despite questions from the two. They thanked the women when they reached the parking area and got out, just as Morale Monitors directed the car farther from the stage.

"Only one pass," Judd said, "we have to split up."

"You take it and find Westin," Lionel said. "I'll stay here and find some kind of transportation."

Judd started off, but Lionel caught his arm. "God help you."

"You too," Judd said.

Lionel moved with the crowd to an area where hundreds of thousands congregated far from the stage. Those with tickets moved forward toward the bright lights while he was herded along a flowery pathway.

Lionel moved as close as he could, but he wasn't able to see much onstage. The program hadn't begun, and people with binoculars sat on others' shoulders to see.

"I think they're about to start," a woman beside him said. She jumped up, trying to see with her binoculars.

A roar rose from the crowd, and Lionel noticed something gleaming in the white-hot lights.

"*C'est une exécution. Ils vont tuer quelqu'un!*" a man shouted.

"What's he saying?" Lionel said to a man beside him.

"It's a guillotine," the man said. "He thinks they're going to perform an execution during the concert!"

TEN

Backstage Pass

THE PASS Judd held didn't have a name, so he clipped it to his shirt and walked confidently around the crowd toward the performer's entrance. He pulled his baseball cap low and strode toward the parked limousines outside the entrance.

The stage was built in a semicircle, the front pointing to the massive crowd that threw beach balls and swayed with prerecorded music. Judd walked by orange fencing to the backstage entrance. He was stopped three times, but when officials saw his pass, they waved him through. A few people had climbed the fence and crowded around security personnel.

One official nearly struck Judd with a nightstick before he saw the pass. "Sorry, sir," the man said, threatening others with his stick as Judd pushed past.

As the door closed, Judd found himself in a darkened area lined with a series of curtains. A concrete path led backstage, where road cases and equipment lined the walls. Judd stayed in the shadows, watching techies make final preparations—testing microphones, tuning guitars, and programming computers.

To his right, along another corridor, was a series of doors. Two were open, and he heard laughter and talking. A little farther were bathrooms. Judd walked swiftly into the darkened men's room, careful not to let anyone see him. He kept the light off and listened through a vent above him that carried the band's conversation.

Where is Westin, Judd thought, *and what do they have planned for him?*

Footsteps approached so Judd scampered to the last stall. He let the stall door stay ajar and stepped onto the seat. The light flickered and Judd shielded his eyes. Someone was pushed into the room and collapsed on the floor, coughing and sputtering like a man drowning.

"The effect should be wearing off soon," a man said as the door swung closed.

"Good." It was Z-Van. "Then he'll feel

every bit of what we have planned for him."
He walked as he talked. "I've been onto you
ever since we left New Babylon. You think I
didn't know that those two convinced you to
become one of *them?*"

"I'm glad you know," Westin said. "I wish
they could have convinced you before you
went over the edge."

"*I* went over the edge? I'm simply doing
the natural, sane thing. Worshiping the true
lord and god of the universe. You, on the
other hand, ran off to the desert and tried to
help Jews escape."

Judd heard a thud and an *oomph* from
Westin, and then Westin vomited. Judd
wanted to look, but he didn't dare move.

"Get him up. He looks groggy," Z-Van
said. "I want him fully awake."

The other man dragged Westin to the first
stall and dunked his head several times.
Westin gasped and Z-Van laughed.

Someone opened the door and said, "Five
minutes."

"We go on when I say we go on!" Z-Van
screamed. "Not a moment sooner."

"Yes sir," the man said.

Westin fell to the floor again and water
splashed all around. Z-Van told the other
man to leave.

"Do you have any idea what power I have?" Z-Van said.

"I suppose you have the power to take my life. . . ."

"The Most High Reverend gave me power—"

"But you don't have any power over my soul!"

"Shut up!" Z-Van yelled, his voice echoing off the walls. "Reverend Fortunato gave me the power to take your life tonight. I said that there would be no need for that. We have a devout follower of Ben-Judah—"

"Of Christ—"

"—whoever, and faced with imminent and certain death, he will choose the only sensible option."

"Which is?"

"Bend the knee to your lord and god and take his mark."

Westin muttered something Judd couldn't hear.

"You will be given that chance tonight, before all those assembled here and who watch by satellite. It will be a spectacle the world will never forget."

"I've read the book," Westin said. "You're going to lose, and so is your so-called god."

Another kick and Westin collapsed. Judd

gritted his teeth. It took all his willpower to keep from going after the singer.

"Tonight you will see who has the power to persuade and who has the power of life and death."

Z-Van banged the door open and yelled at the man outside. "Get someone in there to clean him up. We'll go on in ten minutes."

Lionel borrowed binoculars from a man next to him and focused on the guillotine. It looked small in comparison to the video monitors and banners saluting the Global Community.

He returned the binoculars and turned away, not sure when Judd might return or *if* he would return. "God, I don't know what we're going to do," he prayed silently, "but I ask you to provide some kind of way out of here. And help Judd find Westin before Z-Van uses him for evil."

Lionel walked across another landscaped area and reached a street with people milling about. He noticed a man parked by the road-side reading something. Each cab that passed already had a passenger. Though the print was in French, Lionel recognized the mast-head as Buck Williams's *The Truth*. He had heard of people printing the paper and sending it through co-op sources all around the world.

Lionel moved to get a better look. The man looked up and Lionel gasped. *The mark of the believer!*

Lionel raised his cap, and the man opened his door and stuck out his hand. "It is good to see you, my brother."

"My friends and I are in a tight spot because of this concert," Lionel said.

"How can I help?" the man said.

"We need a ride, but we might be putting your life in danger."

The man smiled. "If my brother in Christ is in trouble, I will help him. I just need to find my son before we leave."

Judd wanted to rush to Westin's aid, but moments after Z-Van left, someone else entered the bathroom. Judd peeked over the top of the stall and saw a man rip Westin's soiled shirt off and put a Four Horsemen T-shirt over his head.

"We have to clean you up before your big debut," the man laughed, "which may be your finale, depending on how you decide."

"I get it," Westin said, "good cop, bad cop.

Z-Van roughs me up, and then you come in and help me."

"Hey, whatever you decide, it's going to be a fabulous show," the man said. "You refuse, you lose your head, and the audience goes wild that there's one less Judah-ite in the world. But if you turn and take the mark, the crowd goes wild because Carpathia's gained another follower."

"I think I'm going to be sick again," Westin said.

The man helped him to the first stall and left him there. "I'll get you something to settle your stomach. We don't want you hurling on Z-Van." He rushed for the door and locked it from the outside.

Westin slouched in the stall. "Give me the strength to do what's right, God."

"He will," Judd whispered.

Westin looked up and his mouth flew open. "How did you—?"

Judd put a finger to his lips. "I'm getting you out of here. I don't know how, but you have to help me."

"I've got a little energy," Westin said. "Whatever they gave me is wearing off."

Footsteps sounded down the hallway. Judd ducked behind the stall and thought about the Morale Monitor he had hurt in Jerusalem. He could think of only one way to get Westin out of Z-Van's clutches, and it might mean hurting this man.

Music exploded from the stage as the man walked into the bathroom. The booming, pounding noise coupled with the roar of the crowd was deafening. Judd inched toward the stall door. The noise lessened as the outer door closed and the man hurried to Westin.

"Drink this," the man said.

Judd slipped behind the thin man, who was just under six feet tall. Westin knelt by the toilet.

The man leaned over. "Are you well enough to take—?" He stopped when he noticed someone behind him.

Judd lowered his shoulder and prepared to level the man, but Westin jumped first, cracking the man's chin with the top of his head. The man fell into Judd's arms like a rag doll, blood pouring from his lip and chin. Judd placed him gently on the floor.

Westin felt for a pulse and grabbed the man's feet. "He's knocked out. He could come around any minute. Help me pull him into the last stall."

Judd did, then switched shirts with the man. "I have the same color hair and basic body type," he said. "Maybe I can get you out of here."

The music blared from the stage so loudly that Judd wondered how anyone in the hallway could hear. Westin turned off the light, and Judd peeked out the door. A guard stood watch a few feet away.

"He's waiting for a signal to bring me onstage," Westin whispered when he closed the door. "We have to take care of him."

"How?" Judd said. "The guy's neck is as big as both my legs."

"We'll jump him."

"Turn on the light," Judd said, running to the last stall and rifling through the man's pockets for keys. The man mumbled, his head lolling to one side. "He's coming around," Judd said as he walked quietly back to the door.

Westin switched off the light and opened the door slightly. "A little help in here!"

The door burst open, and the large man stormed into the bathroom. Westin darted from the dark and tripped him. Judd ran out, holding the door open, but the guard seized Westin's ankle. Finally, Westin broke free and rushed out as Judd closed the door. The guard quickly charged with all his might.

"Get the key!" Westin yelled as he jammed his foot against the bottom of the door. Judd found what looked like the right key, then dropped it as the man inside lunged again.

"Better make this one count," Westin said. "I think he's coming through on the next one."

Judd picked up the key, pushed it in, turned it, and heard the latch click just as the man crashed into the door. The blaring music drowned out his pounding and screaming.

Judd shoved the keys in his pocket, and the two raced for the back entrance. Outside, security guards stopped them, then let them through when Judd showed his pass.

Judd retraced his steps, keeping a wary eye out for members of Z-Van's inner circle. They passed several Morale Monitors caught up in the show, but no one seemed to care about these two hurrying away.

ELEVEN

Onstage Sacrifice

MARK passed the time in the afternoon trying to catch up with questions to the kids' Web site. With the loss of Darrion and the others to the new hideout in western Wisconsin and their search for Vicki, he hadn't had much time to answer e-mails. Though the events of the past few days should have left no room for unbelief, Mark was stunned that many were still undecided. These people had stayed away from public areas where the GC might make them take Carpathia's mark, but they still seemed confused.

Mark wrote another clear message about who Jesus was and how people should respond. He encouraged anyone reading the message to pray the prayer shown at the end of the e-mail and to find another believer who could verify the mark of God.

Mark kept the Global Community News Network on in the background and was surprised by a report from Paris where international rock star Z-Van and his Four Horsemen had begun an evening concert. GCNN dipped into the beginning of the concert, then switched away. Mark flipped channels and found one GC channel covering the event live.

Z-Van appeared in rare form. Whatever physical problems he had from his accident in Israel were gone. He pranced around the stage like a madman, eliciting roars and cheers. When the camera panned to the crowd, Mark couldn't believe it. Hundreds of thousands waved, danced, and cheered the loud music.

Z-Van's message was clear: He celebrated the rise of Nicolae Carpathia and praised the wisdom of the Global Community. He encouraged anyone without Carpathia's mark to take it immediately.

Shelly came in and stood behind Mark, sighing and groaning. "This guy is the best commercial Nicolae's ever had."

Z-Van finished a song, and the crowd went wild. Mark wondered how people at the front of the stage kept from being crushed. Cameras flashed throughout the crowd as Z-Van crossed his arms and rose above the

stage. A white-hot spotlight hit a guillotine at the front of the stage. The razor-sharp blade gleamed and cast its reflection on faces in the crowd.

"Tonight, we celebrate a man of peace and a man who came back from the dead," Z-Van said. His words seemed to have a calming effect as people stopped dancing and waving. "He deserves no less than our complete worship."

Z-Van moved out over the crowd, scanning the faces below him. "But how can we celebrate when there are some of you who have not yet done your duty and sworn your loyalty to our lord and god?"

The crowd was quiet now. A siren warbled in the distance. Z-Van turned and hovered over the stage, then slowly descended.

"How is he doing that?" Shelly said.

Mark didn't have an answer.

Z-Van stood by the sparkling blade of the guillotine and snapped his fingers. "We have at least one with us tonight who has not taken the mark of our beloved leader. Who, as it turns out, still believes in the tired, lifeless God of the Bible. The God of legends and fairy tales and death and destruction. A God who, if we can believe those stories, wiped out the earth with a flood and then says he loves the world. A God who allows all manner of suffering. A God who demands perfection."

Z-Van ran a finger across the blade, and blood dripped from his hand. "We do not serve a god who demands such from his followers. Our kind, loving, and generous deity asks not for perfection, but simply loyalty. Loyalty to the ideals of the Global Community. He asks only that you take a number that can identify you as a lover of peace and that you humbly worship him in spirit and in truth."

Music began and Z-Van sang the title song from his new recording, *Resurrection*. By the end of the song, people stood and cheered. When the music ended, Z-Van turned and waved angrily at someone behind the stage. "Now, you will see firsthand what happens when a man is given one final chance at accepting the love and peace offered through our lord Carpathia, or to continue the charade of following the dead God of the Bible."

A man ran onstage and Z-Van lowered himself. Z-Van's face went from ashen to bright red as the man whispered something in his ear. "No!" Z-Van howled. "Who let him get away?"

The man backed away, his face contorted in fear.

Z-Van dropped to his knees and glared at the crowd. "All right, but someone will make the choice tonight!"

Z-Van flew up, his arms outstretched. Mark thought he was going to mock the crucifixion of Jesus. Instead, Z-Van grabbed a heavy fabric at the back of the stage and pulled it from a statue of Nicolae Carpathia. The eyes of the statue glowed as if on fire. People gasped and some fell to their knees.

"On your knees, every one of you!" Z-Van screamed. "Worship your lord and god!"

Judd held Westin's arm tightly as they ran. The pilot was still woozy from the drugs he had been given, and a red knot was forming on his forehead where he had scuffled with the man in the bathroom.

Judd tried to ignore the music and Z-Van's screams as the two made their way to a street, but when the singer asked everyone to worship the statue of Nicolae, Judd stopped and glanced back. People fell to their knees from the front of the stage to the far reaches of the crowd. Judd and Westin moved into the shadows as Z-Van flew high above the stage.

"Worship your lord and god," Z-Van said.

"Speak his name, and sing of his goodness with me."

Z-Van began a rocky version of "Hail Carpathia." The audience joined in, staggering because of the audio delay from the stage. Applause broke out when they were finished.

"Judd!" someone yelled.

He turned and spotted Lionel standing by a car. Judd helped Westin to the car before the applause ended.

"Where would you like to go?" the man in the front said.

"Anywhere but here," Judd said.

Mark sat, mouth agape, as he watched Z-Van's performance. Others came into the room and took seats. The camera pulled back to show the masses on their knees, some on their faces before the image of Nicolae Carpathia. Morale Monitors and Peacekeepers streamed to the sides of the crowd and took positions with guns.

"Help us identify anyone foolish enough to stand at this holy moment," Z-Van said. "As I said, before this night is through, we will see someone make a choice from this stage. Look around at the people beside you. Check their hands and foreheads. If there is anyone who does not bear the mark of loyalty to the supreme potentate, point them out now!"

A clamor rose as people looked at each other, some laughing, some pointing out the marks. When a shout rang out about thirty yards from the stage, the camera zoomed in on a man standing and pointing. A woman in her twenties cowered on the ground. Another shout came from a cluster behind her, and three more people were found without the mark.

Morale Monitors and Peacekeepers moved in, grabbing the offenders and pulling them toward the stage. Z-Van's eyes twinkled with delight. The band played a mournful tune as eighteen people were led to the front and stood in a line near the guillotine.

"Do you see any believers?" Shelly said.

"There," Mark said, "toward the end of the row."

The crowd hooted and hollered, thinking this was some sort of stunt by Z-Van, but Mark had a sick feeling.

"The believer is talking to the people around him," Colin said.

Z-Van brought the first person forward, the young woman from the front. He pushed her long hair behind her ears and took her face in both hands. "There's no need to be afraid, my dear. We're not here to hurt you. We're here to help you."

Tears streamed down the woman's face, and Z-Van wiped them away. "Why haven't you received the mark of loyalty to your lord and god?"

The woman sobbed. "I've meant to, but I was afraid it would hurt."

The crowd laughed at her, and Z-Van put a hand in the air. "Listen to her. There may be others watching right now who have felt the same way."

"I had a tattoo once," the woman cried, "and it hurt so much. I didn't want to go through that again."

Colin asked Mark to turn the sound down. "Since we know there's a believer in line, I think we ought to pray. These may very well be the last moments of that boy's life."

Colin called Becky into the room, and they all knelt and held hands, praying one by one for a young man they had never met, but who they would no doubt meet in heaven someday.

Judd put his head back on the seat as the man drove through the streets of Paris. Westin had collapsed as soon as he jumped in the car, but Judd didn't know whether it was from exhaustion or fear. They had come close to being hauled onto that stage and Judd knew it.

Lionel introduced the driver, Jacques Madeleine, and explained how the two had met. Jacques hadn't been able to find his son, Perryn, but said he would return for him later. "I can take you to the airport, to my home, or wherever you would like."

"We can't go to the airport," Westin said breathlessly. "They'll be waiting. We'll have to find another way."

"Allow me to take you to my home," Jacques said. "We have a small community of believers. We will be as safe as God allows."

"Why were you sitting by the roadside tonight?" Judd said.

Jacques smiled and looked in the rearview mirror. "My son is very—how do you say?— full of zeal. He told us he would bring a believer home this evening. He will be surprised I have found three."

When they had finished praying, Mark rose and turned up the volume. A few of those standing onstage could speak only French so Z-Van used an interpreter. The others spoke

English fairly well. Every one of the undecided chose the mark of Carpathia, which
was administered onstage by a Global Community representative. People cheered as
each participant took the mark, then wor-
shiped the statue.

Mark noticed the boy with God's mark had
moved to the end of the line. The two
directly in front of him seemed reluctant to
take the mark, but Z-Van convinced them.

Finally, with one person left, people
chanted for more music.

Z-Van lifted a hand and held out a microphone with the other. "And why don't you
have the mark?" he said.

"Oh, I have the mark," the young man
said, "but you're not able to see it."

Z-Van laughed. "An invisible mark for an
invisible follower of our god?"

The young man snatched the microphone
away. "I trust in the only one who can save
you. Not the impostor represented by this
statue, but the man, Christ Jesus, who paid
the penalty for our sins with his very life."

The young man broke free and ran around
the stage like a cat. "If you're watching or
listening right now and you haven't taken
Carpathia's mark, don't do it. If you worship
Nicolae, it means you will never have a
chance to follow the true king. Ask God to

forgive you right now." The young man gave
Tsion Ben-Judah's Web site address, and then
the microphone went silent.

The young man jumped off the stage, and
the crowd swarmed him. When GC authorities had him back onstage, his hands cuffed
behind him, Z-Van sneered. "We know now
why you haven't taken the mark of loyalty.
And every person in this audience knows the
penalty for such crimes against the government of our loving king."

"Guillotine! Guillotine! Guillotine!" the
crowd chanted.

"Your king is not loving or he wouldn't
execute—"

A Peacekeeper clamped the boy's mouth
closed, cutting him off.

"Guillotine! Guillotine! Guillotine!"

Z-Van closed his eyes and drank in the
chant. When the noise died, he turned. "So,
you won't be taking the mark of loyalty?"

The Peacekeeper removed his hand long
enough for the boy to say, "I'll never take
Carpath—"

"Very well," Z-Van interrupted with glee.

GC authorities escorted the boy to the guillotine, made him kneel, and fastened the
device so he couldn't move.

The young man said something in French.

"I think he's praying the Lord's Prayer," Becky said.

A demonic sound emerged from the speakers as the band played another tune.

Z-Van rose above the stage and looked down from near the blade. "The penalty for disobedience against our lord's command is death. May lord Carpathia have mercy on you."

Z-Van pointed to a man at the bottom of the guillotine who tripped a lever and sent the blade plunging. The band whipped the crowd into a frenzy with another wild song.

Mark looked away, too overcome with sadness to watch anymore.

TWELVE

The Chateau

VICKI awoke in the dark and tried to sit up. Her hands had gone to sleep, and she wriggled them to get the blood flowing. She also had to use the bathroom desperately so she groaned loudly. When no one came, Vicki scooted close to the door and banged with her feet.

Vicki thought of the others at Colin's house. She had wanted to drop the information for Tanya at the cave and leave, not get captured.

She felt a rush of fresh air again and looked at the ceiling. The kitchen was next to this room, and there was a vent that went to the top of the cave. Was it possible there was a way out? She struggled but couldn't break free.

Finally, a woman came in and helped Vicki tear the tape from her mouth and hands. She took Vicki to a crude bathroom, which was simply a hole with a board over it. Though some sweet-smelling perfume had been sprayed in the room, the smell was horrible.

"That's the third one we've dug," the woman said. "Hopefully we'll leave before we have to dig another."

"What time is it?" Vicki said.

The woman yawned. "Four in the afternoon. Most people will sleep until eight or nine, and then we'll have breakfast and hear a teaching."

The woman led Vicki back to her room. Vicki noticed the vent in the ceiling that snaked over the stove.

"You don't have to tape me again," Vicki said. "I'm not going to yell or anything."

The woman looked down the hall. "I guess it's hard to breathe, but I still have to tape your hands and feet."

"Please don't tape my hands behind me. They fall asleep."

The woman nodded and taped Vicki's hands and feet with the gray tape. Vicki thanked the woman as the lock clicked.

Judd helped Westin get comfortable as they drove from Paris to the chateau where Jacques and other French believers lived. On the way, Lionel told their story and how long they had been away from their friends in the States.

"You must be anxious to get back," Jacques said.

"We're both ready," Lionel said, glancing at Judd. "For various reasons."

"What's that supposed to mean?" Judd said, smiling.

"Judd has a mademoiselle waiting for him."

"Ah," Jacques said, "I understand."

When Lionel finished their story, he asked Jacques how he had become a believer.

"In my country, the disappearances did not create as much confusion as it did in the rest of the world. We lost less than one percent of our population. But many of us have been searching for answers for years. Some turn to astrology or strange religions. Others seek answers in psychiatry or use drugs to dull their pain. Many don't want to think about what happens when we die, so they pour their lives into today, the now.

"My son has a heart for youth. Many young people have committed suicide. Perryn says Nicolae Carpathia affected young people because he has preached peace and tranquility in the midst of horrible plagues and they have fallen for his lies. I'll make sure you get to meet him before you leave."

"But how did you and your son find out about God?" Lionel said.

"After the disappearances, the war, and the earthquake, I thought of a camp from my childhood. The people who ran it were Christians. I really didn't know much about religion. I couldn't tell you the difference between a Christian, a Jew, or a Muslim. Religion was simply something weird people did in those beautiful churches, synagogues, and mosques.

"But after that brief time at the camp, I knew one thing. These people had something real. They were from different backgrounds and different parts of the world, but they all had discovered what they called a personal relationship with God.

"My parents didn't know it was a Christian camp and when they found out through one of my letters, they came and whisked me away."

"You never went back?" Judd said.

"Not until after the disappearances," Jacques said. "I went to the house alone. It's really an estate on several acres of property, with a soccer field, a beautiful garden, and a chateau—a large house with many rooms. It was deserted. I found clothes at the breakfast table and half-eaten plates of food."

"You must have been scared," Judd said.

"Terrified," Jacques said. "I had heard about the disappearances and the many theories behind them, but I hadn't actually known anyone who had vanished. There was no doubt that these people were gone. But how? Why?

"I went on a search for answers. I scoured the chateau for materials and found several Bibles and pamphlets. They explained more about who God was and what he had done for us in sending Jesus Christ. When I got home, I found a copy of *Global Community Weekly*. One article said that many believed Jesus Christ had returned for his followers and had taken them from the world.

"That's when it all came together for me. I showed the materials to my wife and son, and after some time, they decided I had stumbled onto the truth.

"We prayed together and asked God to help us tell others. We invited friends, family members, and anyone who would listen to our home. Some became believers, but others were hostile. They said we were going against the Global Community with our teaching and threatened to alert the authorities. That's when we moved to the chateau. Now we have to be more careful about the people we invite, but our group is growing, and we see great hope for the future."

They had driven nearly an hour away from Paris when Jacques pulled into the long driveway of the chateau. The headlights illuminated an iron gate covered with ivy. In the middle of a long, finely manicured lawn was a pond with a fountain. The chateau looked like a picture from a travel brochure.

Lionel turned to Judd. "You should bring Vicki to see this."

Judd rolled his eyes and chuckled.

As they pulled up to the circular driveway, a side door opened and a man ran to Jacques and hugged him, tears streaming down his face. He blubbered something in French, and Jacques seemed disturbed.

"What's wrong?" Lionel said.

Jacques furrowed his brow. "It's my son. He was on television tonight."

Vicki worked on the tape, pulling and twisting her hands, but the layers were too strong. Finally, she found the end of the tape and pulled at the corner with her teeth. Slowly it unwound and Vicki freed her hands. She did the same with her feet until she was completely free.

Feeling her way to the back of the room, she found a small table, pulled it to the corner, and crawled on top. With a hand on the wall of the room, she stood and reached the smooth ceiling. It was moist, with a few drops of water running down her arm, and a small shaft of light shone through a crack.

Vicki started digging. The light disappeared and moments later she reached the metal vent. The hole was a foot wide and two feet into the ceiling when a chunk of rock fell to the floor.

She jumped down and searched the room, finding a wooden handle about five feet long, and jammed it into the hole. A shaft of light about the size of a dime shone through. She kept poking with the stick until the hole was a few inches wide.

She stepped off the table and wiped the dirt into the corner. If anyone came in, they would see what she had been doing. But if she worked on the hole another hour or two without being interrupted, there was a chance she could crawl up and out of the hiding place.

Vicki moved to the door and listened. There was no movement throughout the rest of the cave. She wondered what would happen to Tanya if she got away. Would Tanya's father punish the girl? Vicki pushed

the thought from her mind and crawled back
onto the table. She had to get out.

Judd walked inside behind Jacques, Lionel,
and Westin and found a roomful of weeping
people. A woman ran to Jacques and fell into
his arms. They all spoke French, so Judd
couldn't understand them, but the pain on
their faces was enough to tell him something
was terribly wrong.

Westin nodded toward a nearby hallway,
and Judd and Lionel followed.

"Did you understand any of that?" Lionel
said to Westin.

"Enough to know that his son is dead."

"Dead!" Lionel gasped. "What happened?"

"After we left, Z-Van must have gotten
bloodthirsty and decided to go into the
crowd. I don't know how he did it, but they
used the guillotine on that poor kid."

Judd glanced at a television and saw Leon
Fortunato speaking. An impromptu press
conference had been called shortly after
Z-Van's performance.

"Let me say that I am in full support of this
fine young man who represents the ideals of
the Global Community," Leon said from New
Babylon. "Z-Van has been able to communi-

cate through his music on a level the average person can understand. Though his approach is certainly unorthodox, he has the support of the Global Community."

"Was what he did onstage a crime?" a reporter said.

"How could it be a crime to urge others to comply with international law?" Leon said matter-of-factly.

"The beheading though, was it sanctioned by the GC?" the reporter said.

"We did not know all the details of this particular concert, but Z-Van warned us that something shocking might occur. It was his hope that this action would actually save lives in the future and persuade those who refuse to take the mark of loyalty."

"Does this mean the potentate saw the concert?" another reporter said. "And if so, how did he react?"

Cameras whirred in the background. "Yes, His Excellency did see a recording of the event a few moments ago. He was—" Leon searched for the right word—"saddened by the stubbornness of the young man onstage, but he totally supported the action taken. In fact, he even stated that we may have more of these types of events."

Reporters shouted questions, and Leon

raised a hand to quiet them. "You see, our world is changing dramatically every day. Instead of each person finding their own way, we now have the way, the truth, and the life as our guide. Nicolae Carpathia himself is in control, and you can rest assured he will guide us. Victory against the rebels is certain."

Leon stepped away from the podium, and a GCNN anchor cut in. "That ends the press conference with the Most High Reverend Fortunato, reacting to this event viewed live by millions around the world."

Video ran of Z-Van interrogating people onstage. Then the scene cut to him hovering over the guillotine and the blade falling. GCNN showed every gory detail, and Judd turned from the screen.

"That would have been me," Westin whispered. "It should have been."

Wails from the next room saddened Judd. There was no denying that evil forces would stop at nothing to kill followers of the true God.

Vicki worked uninterrupted for another ninety minutes, burrowing and clearing a hole big enough to crawl through. The tiny flow of fresh air felt good on her face as she worked, trying hard not to bang the stick against the vent. She figured if she could wedge herself into the opening, she could crawl up using her arms and feet.

When she had moved all the dirt she could reach, she put the stick under her arm and a foot on the slick surface of the cave wall. Gaining a foothold on a tree root, Vicki hoisted herself into the opening. She grabbed handfuls of soft earth as she pushed with her feet.

Her foot slipped, Vicki lost her balance, and she fell back onto the table. After she made sure she wasn't hurt, she heaved herself back again, putting both feet on the root and grasping the vent for stability. When she was into the opening, she found another foothold and pushed farther.

This is really working, Vicki thought as she inched upward. By holding on to the vent with both arms and pushing with her feet, she neared the top.

She stopped and poked with the stick, her hair filling with dirt and mud. Only a few more feet and she would be outside and headed back to her friends.

A crack sounded behind her, and Vicki first thought it was someone walking into the room. Seconds later, the roof gave way and the earth around her collapsed. Vicki tried to hold on to the vent, but she fell to the floor below.

THIRTEEN

The Shadow of the Cross

VICKI screamed but no sound came from her mouth. She tasted mud and dirt and realized part of the ceiling had fallen on top of her. She knew she had only seconds, but the pressure on her body was so great she could barely move her arms and legs.

Someone shouted from a hundred miles away, or so it sounded. The next few seconds were a blur as someone pulled mud and rocks away, then clutched Vicki's ankles and jerked her out of the pile. She spat out bits of dirt and sucked in air. A gaping hole let in light above.

"Are you okay?" Tanya said, wiping Vicki's face with a wet towel.

Vicki nodded.

Cyrus inspected the ceiling. A hole had opened that was five times the size of the one

Vicki had dug. Trees and rocks stood above in the twilight.

"I was trying to get out," Vicki said. "I had no idea it would cave in."

Cyrus studied the problem. "That vent shaft must have weakened the rest of the ground. Plus, the water seepage didn't help. Get Greg in here so we can figure out what to do."

"Dad, please listen to me. We don't have to stay here anymore."

The man ignored Tanya and waved a hand. "Everybody clear out before the rest of this ceiling comes down." He glared at Vicki. "And see she doesn't get away."

Judd looked through Jacques' family album and saw pictures of his only child, Perryn. The boy's photo was taken at each family function, birthday party, and holiday. Judd thought he looked sad. Mixed with the pictures was Perryn's artwork. The boy had been good, even at an early age, and as he grew older his style and ability showed through. However, the pictures seemed dark. People in the drawings and paintings didn't smile.

Then came the most recent section. There was a dramatic difference. Perryn's face shone with joy. In earlier pictures, the family stood apart with hands at their sides. Now, their arms were draped around each other, hugging and smiling.

At the back of the album, Judd found a painting of a single cross at the top of a hill. Wherever the shadow of the cross touched the landscape, there was life. Plants and flowers bloomed, trees blossomed, animals and people moved about freely in a lush, colorful setting. But the rest of the painting was bleak. Dead trees and plants withered in the darkness. People with bent backs and gaunt faces haunted the canvas. A frightening image at the corner of the painting appeared to be a dragon, chasing and terrorizing people.

At the bottom, in beautiful handwriting, was a verse. Judd recognized John 10:10 at the end and opened a Bible to see what the words were in English. In the passage, Jesus called himself "the good shepherd" and said he would lay down his life for the sheep. In the tenth verse, Jesus said, "The thief's purpose is to steal and kill and destroy. My purpose is to give life in all its fullness."

Judd found the computer room in the chateau and logged on to theunderground-online.com. He copied the picture and sent the file to Vicki and the others with a brief message. *You will hear about a young martyr in*

France who lost his life tonight. Please put this on the Web site. Tell everyone his goal was to see others living in the shadow of the cross.

Sam fell asleep early in Petra on a full stomach and woke a few hours later, rested and fully awake. He had found a spot in one of Petra's many caves near his friend Mr. Stein.

Sam walked in the moonlight over piles of rock that had been blasted apart by GC bombs. He moved toward the computer center, excited at the scene that unfolded around him. People slept in tents, in make-shift buildings, in caves, and even on sleeping bags and blankets scattered about the city. Though Nicolae Carpathia had tried to exterminate these people, they had survived.

The computer building was quiet, with many of the techies sleeping on cots nearby. Naomi wasn't in sight, and Sam assumed she was staying with her father. Sam silently pulled up the kids' Web site and read the latest questions from around the world. Many wanted to know what was going on in Petra after the fiery explosions they had seen on television. The e-mails gave him an idea. Why couldn't he tell them the latest from Petra?

Sam opened a word processing program

and put his fingers over the keyboard. He had never thought of himself as a writer, but the opportunity was too great to pass up.

What do I call this? he thought.

And then it came to him and he moved his fingers over the keys. *The Petra Diaries,* he typed.

God showed up again today in Petra. Let me tell you what happened at ground zero. . . .

Judd e-mailed Chang in New Babylon and asked him to locate any flights the Tribulation Force's commodity co-op might be flying out of France. Jacques and his family remained in the front room, weeping. Judd couldn't imagine the pain of losing a son, and he never wanted to know the feeling.

Chang wrote a quick note back a few minutes later. *Can't help you right now. I think our Trib Force people could be walking into a trap in Greece. Pray for them and for me.*

Judd wondered what was happening in Greece. He knew they were trying to rescue a hostage and that it was a dangerous mission. His thoughts turned to Vicki. He hoped she was safe inside the Wisconsin hideaway, counting the days until his return.

Mark adjusted his night goggles. It wasn't dark yet, but he, Conrad, and Colin wanted to head out as soon as the sky dimmed.

Colin had warned long ago to stay inside, especially at night. With GC satellites flying overhead, who knew what kind of heat-seeking surveillance methods they had. Still, they couldn't leave Vicki alone, and Mark hoped she would still be alive.

Shelly kept watch on the video cameras set up near the woods. Over the past few months, Mark knew she and Conrad had grown closer. Mark hadn't seen it at first. Then Charlie had mentioned something to him.

Becky asked to see Colin in private, and the two went upstairs. Though it was nice to have a place to stay, Mark was becoming increasingly aware that things were getting strained between Colin and the kids. Colin had gone so far as to say that if he and Conrad didn't rest up for the night mission, they wouldn't go.

"Daddy's making us take a nap," Mark had told Conrad as they crawled into their bunks.

"Better keep it down or he'll hear you," Conrad said.

"I don't care. He's treating us like little kids."

"Think of what we've put him through," Conrad said. "He barely came out of Iowa alive, and now we've compromised his safe house."

"Vicki did," Mark said, "not us."

"Hmm. I thought we were a team."

"We were until she ran off and started her personal battle with this group."

"Don't forget, if it wasn't for Colin and his wife, we'd be back at that shelter staring down the wrong end of a GC gun."

"I'm grateful for the help, but I just like it the way it was. At the schoolhouse we didn't have to answer to anyone."

Conrad sat up. "Maybe you shouldn't go tonight. Don't look at me like that. I'm serious. The way you're talking, if we do find Vicki, you'll want to tear her head off."

Mark put his head back and pretended to sleep, but thoughts raced through his mind. Maybe it *was* time for him to leave, perhaps go to the other Wisconsin hideout or join a band of believers in the commodity co-op. There were a lot of ways to fight the enemy besides hiding below ground.

As he started out of the house, Shelly put an arm on Mark's shoulder. "We'll be praying for you."

Vicki stayed with Tanya while a few others worked frantically to shore up the ceiling in the back room. A man with a gun stood watch at the doorway. The light coming through the cave entrance faded, and the lamps took effect.

"Have you talked with anyone other than Ty about what you believe?" Vicki said.

"I've tried. They laughed at me when I told them about the mark on my forehead. My dad won't even speak to me. He says I may be the downfall of the whole group."

A few minutes later, everyone assembled in the meeting area. A woman brought in a large kettle of hot cereal and passed around bowls and spoons. Everyone took some but Vicki.

"For what we are about to receive, make us grateful," Cyrus said.

"Amen," the others said.

Vicki stared at the floor, trying to think of what to say, praying God would give her another chance. She was surprised when Ty raised a hand and stepped toward the table from his spot along the wall.

"I know we haven't had our teaching yet, but I'd like to say something."

"Go ahead," Cyrus said.

Ty's eyes darted from his sister to the

others around the table. "You know I've never questioned anything we've done." He looked at his father. "I've followed what you've said and I've believed it."

"Be careful, boy."

"Tanya's changed. She's different, and it has something to do with what Vicki told her. She and her group have been on the outside this whole time and nothing's happened to them—"

"Sit down," Cyrus said.

"You meant well, Dad, but what if you're wrong? What if we've all been wrong?"

"That's it!" Cyrus thundered. He glared at Vicki and Tanya. "Do you see the trouble you've caused?"

A meek woman at the end of the table spoke so softly Vicki could hardly hear her. "I've seen the change in Tanya too. Maybe we should hear her out one more time."

Cyrus pushed his chair back. "I knew there would come a day when someone would challenge me. I never believed it would be my own flesh and blood."

He walked slowly around the room. "When we came here, we all agreed to the plan. Everyone stays. It's for our own safety. People throughout the world have died, and you've all remained safe. And then this one comes along—" he pointed to Vicki—"and tries to lead you from the true path."

"She's trying to help us," Tanya said.

"Don't talk back to me."

Tanya stood. "Dad, I've respected and loved you. I've tried to be good, but if we're honest, we all know how much we sin. We get angry with each other, we lie, and worse." She glanced at the people around the table. "It's true that you can go to heaven, but not because you do good things. Just one sin is enough to keep you out. But Jesus paid for our sins when he died. We don't have to hide down here and hope we do enough good things. You can know right now you're going to heaven."

"Enough."

"Wait," a man at the back said. "I'd like to hear more."

"Jacob?" Cyrus said.

"We've been cooped up here a long time. How do we know you're telling the truth? Maybe this whole Armageddon thing isn't going to happen now. Maybe it'll be another few years."

"Yeah, you said the battle was going to happen soon," another man said.

Cyrus gritted his teeth and stormed into the next room.

Jacob stepped forward. "Go ahead and talk, Vicki."

Vicki leaned forward. "Tanya did something last night that I did more than three years ago. She prayed and asked Jesus to be her leader and the one to save her from her sin. You can do that too. You simply need—"

A thunderous shot echoed off the walls of the cave, and Cyrus stepped back into the room. Smoke swirled from the end of the shotgun. "We've worked hard to keep this place, and I won't let you come in here and destroy us," he said to Vicki. "Tanya, you'll understand this someday. All of you will. But there comes a time when decisions have to be made for the good of the group."

Everyone sat in stunned silence as Vicki rose.

Mark stopped when he heard the shot. The three had been moving slowly through the woods, retracing their steps from the night before. Now they ran, their night vision goggles bouncing on their faces.

"You think they're hunting again?" Conrad said.

Colin rushed past the ravine and called for quiet.

Mark pushed ahead. He had been so angry at Vicki for going out alone. Now the only emotion he felt about her was fear.

FOURTEEN

Mark's Ultimatum

VICKI'S legs trembled as she stood. Cyrus motioned her away from the others, and Vicki took a step back. Tanya took her hand. "No, Dad, you're not gonna hurt Vicki."

Jacob grabbed Cyrus's arm. "Cy, you know we've believed every word you've said since the first book you wrote. We followed you, we've worked with you, and we've suffered with you."

"Jacob, I don't want to hurt you."

"This young lady hasn't done anything but try to help."

Jacob took a step forward, and Cyrus turned the gun toward him. "I don't care who it is that threatens to break up the group. For the good of all, I'll do what I have to do."

"No, you won't," the bearded man with a gun said. He moved through the doorway and pointed it at Cyrus. "Get her out of here now," he said to Tanya.

Before Vicki could move, Cyrus pushed past her to the bearded man. "So you're going to shoot me, just like that? For a stranger you don't even know?"

"I don't know much about the Bible, but I do know it's wrong to kill."

"Then why would you kill me?"

The man bit his lip. "To defend the innocent. I'd never think of hurting you, Prophet Cy, but when you take arms against young girls like this, it's not right."

Cyrus leveled the gun at Vicki. The bearded man pulled the hammer back on his shotgun and waited. The standoff lasted a few tense seconds. Vicki felt sweat trickling down her forehead.

Cyrus finally walked to the man, grabbed his gun, and wrenched it from his hands. He turned the weapon around, aimed at him, and pulled the trigger.

People screamed, and Vicki covered her ears, expecting to hear another blast. Instead there was only a click and Cyrus laughed. "You don't think I would allow you to have a loaded gun, do you?" He threw the weapon on the floor.

"These have never been loaded?"

"I gave you loaded ones when we went

hunting, but the rest of the time they had blanks in the chambers or no shells at all."

Another man stood. "You haven't trusted us. We trusted you—"

"Everything I've done has been for the good of the group! And it's the same with what I'm about to do."

He seized Vicki by the arm and pulled her toward the narrow entrance.

Mark led the way to the rocks they believed was the hiding place of Tanya's group. Colin pointed to a ledge above some shrubs growing near a cleft, and Conrad carefully climbed to it. Mark peered past the shrubs into the darkness and saw a small opening.

Colin placed him to the right of the entrance and whispered, "I'm going inside. Stay here and let me know if anyone's coming."

Before Colin moved, another shot rang out. The three looked at each other, then raced for the cave opening.

Vicki didn't have a chance to cover her ears as Ty sprang on his father, knocking the man to the floor. The gun went off, pellets penetrating rocks in the ceiling and sending small chunks everywhere. People screamed as the two wrestled.

"Come on!" Tanya yelled.

Vicki vaulted the men and scampered toward the opening with Tanya. Cyrus hollered at them as others wrestled the gun away from him.

Vicki turned a corner and ran into someone.

"Vicki!" Colin said. Mark and Conrad joined them.

"Get out!" Vicki said, grabbing Colin and turning him around.

When they got outside, Tanya pushed them away from the rocks. "Keep going. Dad will be after us."

Colin led the way as they rushed into the night. Conrad held Vicki's hand and Mark held Tanya's. They dodged through trees and found the path past the ravine. In the distance Vicki heard yelling, but they kept going.

Judd, Lionel, and Westin slept in a room with several bunk beds. Judd wanted to tell Jacques how sorry he was about his son, but that would have to wait until morning.

Judd tossed and turned, replaying the scene on television over and over. The look on Perryn's face haunted Judd. He wondered if Jacques would have saved his son if he had stayed in Paris.

Judd awoke in the middle of the night and couldn't get back to sleep. He slipped out of bed quietly and walked downstairs. As he approached the kitchen he found Jacques, his wife, and several others sitting, unable to speak.

Judd turned, but Jacques asked him to come inside. His wife offered Judd something to eat and he politely refused.

"You have heard what happened?" Jacques said.

Judd nodded. "I can't help but think that your helping us kept you from your son."

Jacques pursed his lips. "I admit I have thought the same thing, but my wife brought up a good point. Perhaps my helping you was God's way of sparing my life. If I had waded into that group, my son and I would both have died."

Others around the table agreed. There were men and women, some older, but most middle-aged.

"Perryn is the reason many of us came to Christ," an older woman said. "I was anti-

God, anti-Christian in my upbringing. If you believed in some kind of higher power, it meant you had thrown away your brain."

"How did Perryn reach you?" Judd said.

The woman closed her eyes, as if reliving the moment of her first meeting with Perryn. "He came to my house sometime after the earthquake. I was still able to live in my home, but many of the shingles on the roof were off and the garage was impossible to get into. He asked if I would like them repaired and said the only payment he wanted was for the opportunity to tell me something. I thought he must be trying to rob me, so I sent him away and threatened to call a Peacekeeper."

A few people smiled at her story.

"He came back the next day with tools and some shingles. I stayed outside and watched him every moment. When he finished the roof, he moved to the garage. It took him two days, and when I was sure he wasn't trying to steal things, I made him something to eat.

"He didn't say anything until the job was complete. I handed him a few Nicks for his work and he refused. Then I asked him what he wanted to tell me."

"And he did," Jacques said, smiling through his tears.

The woman nodded. "I screamed at him

and told him to leave. How could he know there was a God who loved me? I had so many problems. So many bad things had happened. How could there be a God? I chased him away, but not before he told me some of the things he believed would happen. One by one, they came true, and I figured he either was a fortune-teller or he really did know God."

Others repeated their stories of meeting Perryn. The more they talked, the sadder Judd became. He would have been a perfect addition to the Young Tribulation Force.

"It doesn't seem right," Judd said during a lull in the conversation. "Why would God take someone so alive, who believed the message so fully?"

"He was the most aggressive soul-winner we had in the group," Jacques said. "He had a vision for this place, that believers from all countries would come here to learn, be refreshed, and go out energized. He was at the concert tonight because he thought God would let him speak to someone."

"I talked with him before he left," a middle-aged man said. "He believed God had something at the concert he wanted him to do."

Perryn's mother looked up through her

tears. She said something in French, and a man brought her a worn Bible. She spoke in her native language and had Jacques translate.

"If Perryn were here," Jacques' wife said, "I think he would give you a favorite verse. This is one he liked to give us when something bad happened."

She turned the pages in her New Testament. Jacques closed his eyes and listened to the words, then translated each phrase. " 'Yes, we live under constant danger of death because we serve Jesus, so that the life of Jesus will be obvious in our dying bodies. So we live in the face of death, but it has resulted in eternal life for you.' "

Judd started to speak, but the woman held up a hand and went further down in the passage. " 'That is why we never give up. Though our bodies are dying, our spirits are being renewed every day. For our present troubles are quite small and won't last very long. Yet they produce for us an immeasurably great glory that will last forever! So we don't look at the troubles we can see right now; rather, we look forward to what we have not yet seen. For the troubles we see will soon be over, but the joys to come will last forever.' "

Judd wiped away a tear and wrote the reference down on a scrap of paper. Those verses perfectly described how every believer had to live at this time in history. He couldn't wait to send the passage to the others in the Young Trib Force.

Vicki took Tanya's hand and scrambled downstairs inside Colin's house. When everyone was safe, Vicki broke down. She couldn't believe what had happened in only twenty-four hours and how her decision to reach out to Tanya had affected everyone.

The others greeted Tanya and welcomed her.

Vicki told them how Tanya had finally believed. "I think her brother and some of the others are close to changing their minds too." She described the scene just before they had escaped. "Once they see that Cyrus is wrong, I'm hoping they'll come to us for some answers."

Tanya was fascinated with the computer setup. She sat glued to Global Community News Network coverage of the latest world events. It had been more than three years since she had seen a television or a computer screen.

Vicki watched the recap of the Petra bombing with interest. Conrad played the footage he had recorded, and she couldn't believe anyone had survived such a blast. Conrad pulled up Sam's Petra Diaries, and the kids read his report together.

While Tanya watched for any sign of her father, Mark gathered the others upstairs. Vicki could tell he was upset.

"I have to say something," Mark said, his face drawn and tight. He looked at Vicki, then glanced away. "I'm really glad you're back, and I'm happy about Tanya. I don't want you to misunderstand what I'm about to say."

Vicki put a hand on his arm. "Let me start. I need to apologize for what I—"

Mark held up a hand. "I know you didn't mean to get caught out there. I'm sure you had good intentions, but this has happened too much. After the first time you went out, I thought it was clear . . ."

"I know. I felt guilty that I hadn't been able to convince Tanya of the truth. Aren't you glad she responded? She's a believer now."

"That doesn't excuse what you did. I can't go on without saying or doing something, and that's led me to a hard decision."

"Which is?" Vicki said.

"We can't stay together and not be accountable." Mark looked at the others. "And it's clear I'm the one who has the problem with this." He took a deep breath. "Either I need to leave or Vicki needs to go."

FIFTEEN

Confrontation

Sam looked for Mr. Stein but was unable to find him in the hustle and bustle of the Petra morning. Some people were just stirring, gathering manna and water for breakfast.

Finally, Sam found Mr. Stein praying with a few others in a rocky nook near one of the high places above the city. The men prayed for the safety of pilots and drivers transporting materials to Petra, and for craftsmen who could help build more shelters for families and individuals.

Everyone spoke about the miracle from the day before. Those who still had questions seemed anxious to hear the teaching from Dr. Tsion Ben-Judah scheduled for later in the day.

Sam noticed a few men carrying what looked like a huge, white flag to the top of one of the high places. When the men had the canvas spread out in a shady area, it stood several stories high. To Sam's surprise, an image flickered on the material, and a copy of *The Truth* cyberzine flashed on the makeshift screen. People cheered the report of what had really happened in Petra the day before. Another story concerned brave believers in Greece who had chosen to fight Global Community forces trying to catch members of the Tribulation Force.

Sam moved to the computer building and found Naomi. She was smiling, busy at one of the tiny laptop computers. "Last night, the elders asked Dr. Ben-Judah to stay in Petra and transmit his teachings from here rather than go back to the States. He asked the elders, one of which is my father, to find young people with gifts of administration and organization to help set up a government here."

"We do have at least three more years before the return of Christ," Sam said.

Naomi saved the file she was working on and moved through the room. "And there are so many things to be done. Dr. Ben-Judah wants us to help our brothers and sisters around the world. He says Carpathia and his followers will become more and more upset, and many believers will die. But we can use our resources here to frustrate Antichrist."

"How are we going to do that?" Sam said.

"Dr. Ben-Judah sees us moving supplies

around, telling people about safe houses, and putting believers in touch with each other."

"Like a massive rescue effort—"

"Yes, all done from right here in Petra, where we will be safe and God will provide food, water, and clothing until Christ's return."

"Wow. And we'll continue to tell people about God?"

"Definitely. In fact, Dr. Ben-Judah has a new message."

"Tell me."

"We are in the middle of the last seven judgments of God. There are twenty-one in all. And even though this is a time of God's wrath, Dr. Ben-Judah says this is a time in which he will teach about God's mercy."

"Mercy? With people dying left and right and Carpathia on the rampage?"

"Yes, he says he will spend the rest of his time in Petra teaching about the love of God."

"I can't wait to hear it."

Judd woke up late and found Westin and Lionel in one of the main rooms watching the latest news from New Babylon. A special report was promised within the hour. Judd asked about Jacques and the others.

Lionel said they had gone out early. "I don't think any of them went to bed."

Judd phoned Chang and left a coded message for him to return the call. He wanted to see if there was any word from Chang about getting a flight from France.

A few minutes later the phone rang, and Chang seemed out of breath. "I don't know where to begin. I've just gone through the longest night of my life. It took some fast computer work, but I found out our people in Greece were walking into a trap."

"And you stopped that?"

"All four of our people got out of there, with some divine help."

"What do you mean?"

"Our people were on a runway with a GC plane staring them down. Michael appeared on the plane and got them out of there."

"You mean the angel Michael?"

"Yes. I hacked into the transmission between the GC plane and the tower, and the pilot reported a light so blinding that they couldn't see the Trib Force plane. You should have heard them screaming. God was at work."

Judd was thrilled but not surprised. If God could deliver a million people from bombs in Petra, he could help others in trouble. But would he help Judd and Lionel get home?

"I had a major scare later in the night,"

Chang continued. "I was listening to Nicolae talk with one of his top people, and they said they definitely believe the security breach is inside the palace."

"They're talking about you?"

"Yes. And later my screen flashed like someone was trying to get through my firewall, but I found out it was only a computer whiz in Petra searching the palace system."

Judd explained what he and Lionel had experienced the night before and asked for help getting back to the States.

"I'm working on a media thing right now. Make sure you watch the GC news special coming up. I'll get back to you about your flight home. In the meantime, stay hidden and take care."

"Chang, you can't stay there."

"I'm willing to do my work during the day, then do what I'm really called to during the night."

"For how long?"

"For as long as God protects me."

Judd went back to the television and sat by Lionel. Reports from around the world of nighttime raids seemed to thrill reporters. Though troops in the Middle East had been decimated, other Morale Monitors and the Peacekeepers seemed energized by news of the

crackdown on those without the mark of
Carpathia. People were even punished for not
worshiping Nicolae's image three times a day.

"Oh no," Lionel said, looking at Judd,
"here comes your buddy."

Leon Fortunato appeared on-screen and
warned everyone with Jewish ancestry who
refused to worship Carpathia. "Oh, they shall
surely die, but it is hereby decreed that no
Jew should be allowed the mercy of a quick
end by the blade. Graphic and reproachful as
that is, it is virtually painless. No, these shall
suffer day and night in their dens of iniquity,
and by the time they expire due to natural
causes—brought about by their own rejec-
tion of Carpathianism—they will be praying,
crying out, for a death so expedient as the
loyalty enforcement facilitator."

Next came an anchorman who revealed the
shocking news that the two bombs and the
missile dropped on Petra had missed their target. "The two pilots were attacked by the rebels
and were killed by a surface-to-air missile."

Judd shook his head. "That's so lame. The
world knows what really happened."

Nicolae Carpathia was shown biting his
lip, his chin quivering. "While there is no
denying that it was pilot error, still the
Global Community, I am sure, joins me in
extending its deepest sympathy to the surviv-

ing families. We decided not to risk any more personnel in trying to destroy this stronghold of the enemy, but we will starve them out by cutting off supply lines. Within days, this will be the largest Jewish concentration camp in history, and their foolish stubbornness will have caught up with them.

"Fellow citizens of the new world order, my compatriots in the Global Community, we have these people and their leaders to thank for the tragedy that besets our seas and oceans. I have been repeatedly urged by my closest advisers to negotiate with these international terrorists, these purveyors of black magic who have used their wicked spells to cause such devastation.

"I am sure you agree with me that there is no future in such diplomacy. I have nothing to offer in exchange for the millions of human lives lost, not to mention the beauty and the richness of the plant and animal life.

"You may rest assured that my top people are at work to devise a remedy to this tragedy, but it will not include deals, concessions, or any acknowledgment that these people had the right to foist on the world such an unspeakable act."

Not long after Nicolae's message, Judd noticed audio covering up the GCNN anchor's voice. "Chang told me something was going to happen. Listen to this."

Though GCNN reporters tried to speak over the audio, they could not override Chang's bold actions. He played a recording of Suhail Akbar talking with the pilots. It was clear that the pilots hadn't missed the target and hadn't been shot down by the Petra rebels. The GC tried to call the recording a hoax, but everyone heard Suhail Akbar call for the execution of the pilots.

Judd heard voices outside and joined Jacques and the others from the chateau on the back lawn.

Jacques smiled and put an arm around Judd. "We will not be able to bring our son's body home because the GC would detain us, so we're holding Perryn's memorial service now."

"I'll get my friends," Judd said.

Vicki had been crushed by Mark's words. She understood his anger and felt upset about her own actions, but to threaten to leave or throw her out didn't make sense.

Vicki wanted to defend herself, to say she had put up with a lot of bad behavior from Mark. But Vicki knew she had made a mistake, had gone against the wishes of the group, and needed to sit quietly and think things through.

What would Judd say if he were here? Vicki wondered. Would he agree with Mark? Perhaps Mark had talked with Judd about what she had done.

Vicki went to her room and sat alone. A series of events had left Colin's home and the small band of believers vulnerable. Would Cyrus's people come to them for help? Would they try to hurt them for taking Tanya away?

Vicki asked God for direction. Though he had shown himself mighty in the past few days, Vicki felt God's silence. She didn't know what to do or if she should do anything.

A few minutes later she walked into the meeting room. The others quieted as she stepped forward. "Okay, I've thought it over." She looked at Mark. "You're right. I ought to be punished in some way, so I guess I'll be leaving the group."

Sam shook with anger as he watched the lies of the Global Community paraded on the huge screen. People hissed and booed at Nicolae Carpathia but cheered when they heard the truth about how the pilots really died.

Thousands had gathered near the screen,

while others watched from high perches. A ripple of excitement ran through the crowd as a lone figure climbed onto a rock outcropping overlooking the vast audience. The video feed went silent, as did the group, when Micah raised both hands high and began to speak in a loud voice.

"It is my great pleasure and personal joy to once again introduce to you my former student, my personal friend, now my mentor, and your rabbi, shepherd, pastor, and teacher, Dr. Tsion Ben-Judah!"

The crowd cheered. Sam wiped away a tear, happy that he was in this place at this time—the safest place on earth for a Jewish believer. He wondered what new teaching Tsion would give this vast audience and how the next three years would treat his friends, Judd, Lionel, and the rest of the Young Tribulation Force.

Judd stood at the back of the group of mourners who surrounded a flower bed Perryn had planted. Each person prayed prayers of thanksgiving for Perryn's life. Jacques tried to read Scripture but couldn't.

Another man took the Bible and read verses of comfort, then knelt by the flowers. "Before his death, Jesus said, 'The time has come for the Son of Man to enter into his glory. The truth is, a kernel of wheat must be planted in the soil. Unless it dies it will be alone—a single seed. But its death will produce many new kernels—a plentiful harvest of new lives.' "

The man looked up at the group. "Just as these flower seeds were planted and died and bloomed in such splendor, so our Perryn will give glory to God. We may never know until heaven what his example on that stage meant for eternity. We mourn his loss. We grieve not being able to say good-bye. But we rejoice that in three short years, we will be reunited because of the one who died, rose again, and is coming again. Jesus Christ."

"Amen," the group said.

Judd could hardly contain the emotion. He hadn't known Perryn, hadn't ever spoken with him, but he felt such a bond with the young man and his friends.

While the others moved inside, Judd walked to the back of the yard to a utility shed filled with gardening tools and lawn equipment.

Jacques met him there and put an arm around him. "Do not blame yourself, Judd. God is never surprised at our suffering or at death. He knows the end from the beginning, and though I don't understand, I do trust him."

Judd nodded and leaned against the building.

"I want to ask you a question. Think about your answer. Your presence here is not by mistake. And I sense in you—and in your friends—the same spirit in my son. A desire to follow God wholeheartedly and tell others of him."

Jacques took hold of Judd's shoulders. "Perhaps you were sent here by God to finish the work Perryn began. Would you consider staying until his vision is complete?"

ABOUT THE AUTHORS

Jerry B. Jenkins (www.jerryjenkins.com) is the writer of the Left Behind series. He owns the Jerry B. Jenkins Christian Writers Guild, an organization dedicated to mentoring aspiring authors. Former vice president for publishing for the Moody Bible Institute of Chicago, he also served many years as editor of *Moody* magazine and is now Moody's writer-at-large.

His writing has appeared in publications as varied as *Reader's Digest*, *Parade*, *Guideposts*, in-flight magazines, and dozens of other periodicals. Jenkins's biographies include books with Billy Graham, Hank Aaron, Bill Gaither, Luis Palau, Walter Payton, Orel Hershiser, and Nolan Ryan, among many others. His books appear regularly on the *New York Times*, *USA Today*, *Wall Street Journal*, and *Publishers Weekly* bestseller lists.

Jerry is also the writer of the nationally syndicated sports story comic strip *Gil Thorp*, distributed to newspapers across the United States by Tribune Media Services.

Jerry and his wife, Dianna, live in Colorado and have three grown sons.

Dr. Tim LaHaye (www.timlahaye.com), who conceived the idea of fictionalizing an account of the Rapture and the Tribulation, is a noted author, minister, and nationally recognized speaker on Bible prophecy. He is the founder of both Tim LaHaye Ministries and The PreTrib Research Center. He also recently cofounded the Tim LaHaye School of Prophecy at Liberty University. Presently Dr. LaHaye speaks at many of the major Bible prophecy conferences in the U.S. and Canada, where his current prophecy books are very popular.

Dr. LaHaye holds a doctor of ministry degree from Western Theological Seminary and a doctor of literature degree from Liberty University. For twenty-five years he pastored one of the nation's outstanding churches in San Diego, which grew to three locations. It was during that time that he founded two accredited Christian high schools, a Christian school system of ten schools, and Christian Heritage College.

Dr. LaHaye has written over forty books that have been published in more than thirty languages. He has written books on a wide variety of subjects, such as family life, temperaments, and Bible prophecy. His current fiction works, the Left Behind series, written with Jerry B. Jenkins, continue to appear on the best-seller lists of the Christian Booksellers Association, *Publishers Weekly*, *Wall Street Journal*, *USA Today*, and the *New York Times*.

He is the father of four grown children and grandfather of nine. Snow skiing, waterskiing, motorcycling, golfing, vacationing with family, and jogging are among his leisure activities.

The Future Is Clear

Check out the exciting Left Behind: The Kids series

BOOKS #35 AND #36 COMING SOON!

Hooked on the exciting
Left Behind: The Kids series?
Then you'll love the dramatic audios!

Listen as the characters come to life in this theatrical
audio that makes the saga of those left behind
even more exciting.

High-tech sound effects, original music,
and professional actors will have you
on the edge of your seat.

Experience the heart-stopping action and
suspense of the end times for yourself!

Three exciting volumes available on CD or cassette.